MORTAL SOULS

Amy Hoff

Erebus Society

Erebus Society

First published in Great Britain in 2018
by Erebus Society

First Edition

ISBN: 978-1-912461-12-7

www.erebussociety.com

For Linn, my favourite cryptid.

You are so weird.

TABLE OF CONTENTS

About the Author

Amy Hoff spent years travelling across the United States, living out of cars and cheap motels. She was a weightlifter and street-fighter, collecting monster legends across the country. Eventually she left the USA and continued travelling around the world. She was educated in Scotland and specialised in Scottish history, literature, and folklore. She is now a folklorist and historian whose primary research interest is monsters. She has never owned more than what can fit into a backpack and a suitcase.

CHAPTER ONE

Yoo Min stared out at the rain and mist shrouding Glasgow. She sipped her tea, and considered how the grey tendrils wrapped around the dim streetlights as the dawn approached. The city glowed a soft orange in the darkness, a Victorian memory reminiscent of Sherlock Holmes and the hansom-cab grey streets of London in popular imagination.

Yoo Min was very, very old.

She thought of the night she had left Seoul, that city of colour and sound, before coming here, to this drab and grey colourless place.

Yoo Min was a *gumiho*, the nine-tailed fox woman that ate the livers of handsome men. Lately she had been hungrier, walking down the streets of the city, in the night markets as she passed by the young men in silence. She could *scent* them, on the soft winds that breathed through the urban capital. She walked on, just another woman on the busy night streets of Seoul.

The beautiful gumiho sighed. Ninety-nine years, seven months, and two days – and counting. No one even knew if it would work. The oldest legends said that a gumiho denying herself the taste of a man's liver would one day become human. She would soon find out. It was trying at times, particularly when she was bored. A cruel diet, as like starvation as not.

Distracting herself from her hunger, her mind was lost in memory, as the neon lights surrounded her and the steam rose from the food at the countless little restaurants and night markets.

The men still noticed her, and looked her way. They smiled,

unaware their flirtations were calling to a shark, dead-eyed and moving slow, purposeful, quiet, through the streets of the city.

Yoo Min smiled, and the men hurriedly looked away. She had strange sharp teeth and she smiled far too wide. She was a pretty girl, and a nightmare thing.

They left her alone, for the most part. Some kind of ancestral memory, because most of them did not remember the folklore enough to know better, anymore. Still, they let her be.

There were few things that surprised her, not the wash of time nor the cruelty of men.

Tae Pyeong had been a surprise.

GYEONGJU
SILLA KINGDOM
640 AD

The wind blew the fragrant scent of spice viburnum through the streets, and through the small houses near the palace. A beautiful girl ran through the darkness, past bunches of flowering *mugunghwa*. Her hand was placed over her mouth, hiding a smile, and her eyes lit up even in the deep twilight of late evening. She made sure she hadn't been followed, and turned up a path to the hill littered with flowers.

Yoo Min climbed to the top of the hill, and looked out across the valley of the city. Gyeongju, the great capital of the Silla Dynasty, would soon know untold riches under the reign of Queen Seondeok.

She waited, almost holding her breath, smiling. She would know the sound of his footstep anywhere.

Lithe, slim, lovely – the boy was like no one she had seen in her long, long years. A romantic, skilled in the arts, including those of love. His talents were meant for the queen alone, but he had chosen her instead. If he were discovered, his life would be forfeit.

He would give up everything for her.

Tae Pyeong was an idealist and a romantic. He believed his

love would carry them through any obstacle. They had heard of faraway exotic places. Speaking in whispers late at night, he had told her they could travel together to see the famous cities of the world.

Her breath caught as she heard steps on the path. She turned.

Smiling at her, love shining from his dark eyes, Tae Pyeong was so intensely beautiful that wars might be started over the right to gain his favour. Yoo Min had never seen his like in the thousands of years she had been alive. Beautiful was not a word that sufficed, in any language.

The *Hwa Rang* – *flower boys* – of Queen Seondeok were famous. Chosen for their beauty, they were trained in every aspect of the gentle arts. Also called *Hyangdo, fragrant ones* or *incense men,* they were taught some of the military arts, but their main purpose was to serve as the cultured and educated harem of the queen.

Tae Pyeong was a special favourite.

He bowed low before Yoo Min, his forehead touching the ground. She gently lifted his chin so he could look into her eyes, and they embraced. He kissed her.

"Are you ready?" he asked.

She nodded.

"Are you afraid?" he asked, "To leave here?"

She nodded again.

"Yes," she replied, "I have known no other life."

"You deserve more," he said.

Yoo Min smiled at his naïveté. She deserved nothing, and she knew it. She knew she had no right to him, and she knew how dangerous it was, but she had been selfish; her love had inspired a greed in her heart she had not known before.

"And what of you? Will you not miss the arms of Seondeok?" Yoo Min asked, already knowing the answer.

"When I am in your arms, all else is forgotten," he said, and smiled.

Her heart felt as though it might break from happiness.

SEOUL, SOUTH KOREA
MODERN DAY

Yoo Min walked through the subway, waving her mobile phone at the barrier. It let her through immediately. She walked up to the touch screen on the wall, to model in the mirror as clothes were fitted to her image and she ordered a few dresses. She remembered running down that Gyeongju street, hiding her smile, in another time. Seoul had risen from the ashes of the Korean War to become a technological megacity with an everyday science fiction reality, even in comparison to the rest of the world. Seoul was Byzantium, Bohemian Paris, Rome at its height.

Still, she could feel the old hunger in her heartbeat, whenever one of the well-dressed descendants of the *Hwa Rang* passed her on the street. In the modern age, the men had embraced the flower boy aesthetic once again, and Yoo Min was finding it more and more difficult to deny herself. She had not been hungry like this in centuries. Tae Pyeong had been on her mind a great deal lately, enough that his memory had been distracting her from her duties at Hanguk Interpol. They had recommended a transfer to a place where the men could not possibly tempt her, particularly in comparison to the visions that filled the city streets of the Korean capital.

She stood on the hill above Seoul, watching the city lights, as she had once waited on a hill in Gyeongju, for a boy whose love she did not deserve.

She touched the piece of Tae Pyeong's rib bone on a silver chain around her neck, inlaid with the heron symbol of immortality.

Blood.
Yoo Min, I love you. I forgive you.
Tae Pyeong.
Like Adam, I am made from him.

❦ CHAPTER ONE ❦

CALEDONIA INTERPOL
GLASGOW, SCOTLAND

Leah Bishop regarded the slim young man in the impeccable suit through the steam rising from her teacup. His large brown eyes, fringed with dark lashes, gave him a mournful look; the hangdog expression of a seal staring out from the water. His extreme etiquette and formality was evident in his spotless tailcoat, gloves, and the gleaming chain of his pocketwatch. Despite his resemblance to a seal, he was quite handsome, his great dark eyes expressive and bright. When he turned to look at Leah, one eyebrow archly rose.

"Yes?" asked Dorian Grey.

"Staring contest," said Leah, grinning. Dorian looked down his aristocratic nose at his partner.

"Is that so?" he asked.

"You've lost already, about ten times," she said.

An older man walked into the room, grizzled and dignified in his old leather coat. He had piercing blue eyes and a threatening manner, but it belied a strong and loyal heart beneath.

"So, how are you two wasting time?" Chief Benandonner asked.

Leah made a disgusted noise and rolled in her chair.

"Aww, Chief, there's nothing happening in our world," said Leah, "Plenty in the human world, but the faeries have been nice to each other."

Dorian stirred.

"I must agree with Miss Bishop," he said, "Things have been very quiet of late. There's nothing for us to do."

"What about Sebastian?" asked the chief.

"We've looked," said Leah, "the trail ends – completely. He knows what he's doing. I do miss Geoffrey, though."

"Always more fish in the sea, Miss Bishop," said Dorian, "and I would know."

"I've got horrible taste in men," said Leah.

"Indeed."

"You're not supposed to *agree* with me!"

"Did Sebastian say anything to you?" Chief Ben interrupted.

"Only that stupid thing about Dylan," said Leah. Ben turned to look at her.

"What's that?" he said.

"He said something like... he's not the real problem. That the Guardian was killed – or that Dylan would only be 'called' if a Guardian was killed. Then he told me to protect his city, the arrogant –"

Chief Ben's presence filled the room. He seemed to become the giant he was.

"*Detective Inspector Bishop*, if you even deserve that title, do you not realise what he was telling you? You were the one with the brilliant idea to listen to the ravings of a madman – because they weren't ravings, after all. And yet you miss this?"

Leah stared at him, bewildered.

"*Sebastian didn't kill the Guardian.* The other faeries, sure – but if he thinks of Glasgow as 'his city' he certainly isn't going to take down one of the Guardians that protect it from outside forces. There's something we're missing, because when Tearlach appeared on Saturday night in front of Dylan, he'd only just seen one of the Attendants killed."

"A moment," said Dorian. "Now that you mention it, I realise that the night Aonghas claimed he was kidnapped was also a Saturday night. Saturday nights are like the twilight times to the Glasgow fae. We mirror the city, and the people within it."

"Wasn't Aonghas taken on Sauchiehall?" asked Leah, "And Tearlach found Dylan there as well?"

"That's what I like to see," said Ben, clapping Leah on the shoulder, "my detectives. Detecting. It's what I pay you for. You'll let me know if you figure anything out."

Ben went into his office and shut the door behind him. Leah and Dorian didn't notice him leave.

"There may be something to this," said Leah, "but we'd need to find out if anything else particularly magical happened on that Saturday night, on Sauchiehall Street."

"I don't know, Leah, it's very thin," said Dorian.

"You'd know," she said, looking at his lithe figure, "but I think there might be something in it."

"I agree there is something strange going on," said Dorian, "and we were so caught up in Sebastian – and Magnus– we missed the most obvious clue. Listen to the madman, he isn't always a fool."

"I think Paul McCartney wrote a song about that," said Leah.

"I'm sure I've no idea who that is," said Dorian.

"Oh, come on! Greatest pop band the world has ever known, he wrote Mull of Kintyre, lived in Scotland himself? I once almost got into a fistfight at a pub over him," she said.

"Indeed? Was he one of your lovers?" asked Dorian.

"I'm about to get in a fistfight with you in a minute," said Leah, "I *know* you know who I mean."

"Newfangled music," said Dorian, shaking his head.

"All right, then, Little Lord Fauntleroy," said Leah, "how about we go ask some questions?"

"Do not compare me to the *bourgeoise*, madam," said Dorian, "passionate scoundrels, the lot of them."

"You know, I really have no idea how you survive in this city," said Leah.

Dorian allowed a slight smile to crease his features.

Glasgow was dark, and the streetlamps glowing gold reminded Leah of Victorian London in the mist and rain – or even, strangely, Paris. The city could be beautiful at times. She and Dorian walked together, incongruous in the crowd – a modern girl with a Victorian gentleman.

They located the door they had been looking for. Leah placed a white hand on the red door, pushing it open easily. The security system had broken long ago.

The long yellow hallway was lit with a single pale lamp. Graffiti on the walls and their cold, hollow footsteps on the concrete floor completed the feeling of despair in the place, and the need to escape. Escape in any way possible.

They turned the corner, where on the concrete stairs lay a woman drained. Her face was aged, her teeth falling out and her hair stringy. It was a very familiar sight to any Glaswegian – the heroin addicts in the city had found the secret places in the outer regions where unlocked doors provided shelter for the next hit.

They knew the angel was there before they saw him.

The beating of his wings. The feathers that graced the floor, falling like a cloak behind him.

A young man with an honest face, dressed in a familiar track suit, was crouched in front of the woman. Seraph wings of a brilliant white sheltered her, as though he were holding her in his arms. The wings wrapped around her, offering comfort and solace, a strange stained-glass window image in a council house close reeking of urine and despair in one of the darkest parts of Glasgow.

He turned to look at them as they approached, and he stood up out of respect, his wings retracting and vanishing until he looked like any other person on the street. He nodded at them. His eyes were sad.

"Sorry to interrupt," said Leah.

"'S fine," said Dylan, "yer awrite, she's been gone fer some time. I thought a last beau'iful dream of angels might help her rest easier."

"Dylan," said Dorian, more gently than Leah was accustomed to hearing, "you cannot save everyone."

Dylan looked at him in defiance.

"The Guardians have neglected this place too long," he said decisively, "and this is the only way change comes – one person at a time. Do you know what it's like to clean up thousands of years of mess?"

"We have come to ask you some questions," said Dorian.

"Oh? Am I a suspect then?" said Dylan.

"No," said Leah, "but we're trying to find out what Sebastian meant in his last phone call – that you wouldn't have been called if a previous Guardian hadn't been taken. Do you know who it was? The Guardian you replaced?"

Dylan thought for a moment.

"Well, there are six of us," he said, "I dinna hae Attendants yet, because I'm young. The others do. There's myself, Aonghas, the Angel, the Lomond Monster, the Nuckelavee, and..."

He looked puzzled, and shook his head.

"I dinnae much about the sixth," he said, shrugging.

"Anyway," said Dorian, "we're going to have to question the others."

"Well, Aonghas doesn't know anything," said Dylan loyally, "besides, he'd have told me if he did."

"Maybe we should start putting the Guardians on the pay-roll?" asked Leah as they departed, leaving Dylan at his post, overlooking Glasgow Green.

Dorian sniffed.

"What I want to know," said Leah, "is why bad things happen, even when there's a Guardian sitting right there. Glasgow Green is famous for being a nasty part of the city, although I'm sure King James wasn't thinking it would end up like this when he first created it."

"I wish I knew," said Dorian. "Sometimes things just happen."

Leah gave him a sharp look, but he did not appear to notice.

They had questioned everyone they could think of. Dorian pointed out that if they were to put everyone on the payroll they would have to pay every faerie in Glasgow.

"It looks like there is only one thing left," said Dorian.

"What's that?"

"Leaving the city."

"Shame about her, though," said Dylan, returning his attention to the body on the staircase.

"She was dying. Of an overdose," Leah pointed out, "there wasn't anything you could do."

"No," said Dylan, fixing Leah with a challenging stare, "Wasnae heroin."

"Pardon?" asked Dorian.

"Dunno," said Dylan. "Wasnae drugs. Not a kind I've ever

seen, anyway. I think she was ill."

Dorian moved closer, intrigued.

"Ill? What do you mean?" he asked.

Dylan shrugged, and then lifted the woman's arm. Her hand was black from fingertips to elbow.

"Dinnae ken," he said. "Never seen anything like it before."

Dorian recoiled.

"I have," he said sharply.

Turning swiftly to Leah, he began to bundle her out the door.

"Dorian, what –"

Dorian spun on his heel. The blood had drained from his face and his eyes were bright.

"We need to get you out of here, Miss Bishop," said Dorian. "*Right now.*"

***

In the police station, Lee Yoo Min walked into the holding cell area of the Deeps, the part of Caledonia Interpol's underground prison wrapped in the most powerful magic. She had been tasked to deliver meals to the prisoners who were awaiting trial at the faerie tribunal. She saw that there were not many cells empty; this city, unlike her own, apparently had its share of offenders.

She pushed the trolley through the hallway, depositing meals, annoyed. She was also a detective, and this was brownie work. She was five thousand years old; she wasn't a rookie. However, Chief Ben had indicated that the usual woman was off sick – a warrior faerie named Aoife who also served as one of the two receptionists at Interpol, along with Lindsey, a pixie, it was said, that some of Scotland's most famous folksongs had been written about. She'd come to them via Lidl, where Ben had noticed her behind the counter, boredly ringing things up, and she'd jumped at the chance to join the fae police.

Well, at least it isn't Lidl, Yoo Min groused to herself. Still, she supposed it was always best to show willing at work.

As Yoo Min was considering this, consoling herself with memories of former strength and feats of horror, she absent-mindedly pushed a meal through the grate of a door. Lying on his side with his back to her, she saw a beautiful form and a cascade of brown and golden curls that had fallen over a shoulder. The form stirred, and rolled over to look at her. The ivory face, the large eyes with a natural kohl-like outline, the darkly arched brows, and the lazy smile when he saw the beautiful woman standing before him, spoke to her heart in the same way that a bar filled with various liquors glitters like gemstones to an alcoholic. Then the man stood, and sauntered over to her, walking like a cat. He placed a graceful hand on the bars, and she stared up into the widest brown eyes she had seen in her long life.

"Hello," he said, smiling down at her, his voice gentle and insinuating. "I don't think we've met."

She backed away, turning very red in the face. She shook her head. The beautiful man gave her a puzzled look.

"*No no no no no*," she said fiercely, almost to herself, the *hunger* rising up in her with a vengeance. She looked at him one more time, as if to make sure he was real, and then ran up the stairs.

Magnus Grey stared after her, and laughed.

CHAPTER TWO

The phone at the Caledonia Interpol front desk was ringing off the hook.

"Where the *hell* is that receptionist?" said Chief Ben. Yoo Min stood next to the desk.

In a bright burst of energy, Aoife appeared. She sat down and picked up the receiver.

"Caledonia Interpol," she said.

"You just can't get good help these days," Chief Ben said to Yoo Min. Aoife sent him a scalding look.

Leah and Dorian walked into the office. They were surprised to see a young Korean woman talking to the Chief.

"Who's this?" asked Leah.

Yoo Min turned around and bowed to them.

"My name is Lee Yoo Min," she said, "I will be working with you."

Leah raised an eyebrow at the Chief. He shrugged.

"Someone had to replace Magnus," he said, "Sorry, Dorian."

Dorian nodded, although his mouth tightened and his jaw twitched.

"Quite all right," he said, "Chief, there's an emergency."

"Oh?" asked the Chief, "What is it?"

"A woman just died of the Black Death in a Bridgeton close," said Dorian.

The city had grown still, which Glasgow never was. There was a kind of fear in the streets, a fear in only the darkest quarters. Death crept among them there, but no one took much notice; no one ever did, besides the Guardians, and a young angel in a tracksuit whose halo shifted askew above his head.

What was it to the other denizens of the city if the poor and drug-addicted perished? *Their fault, really*, words that were almost but not quite said over tea in their comfortable offices as rain lashed down the windows. The neds were an annoyance, bringing violence, begging, a nuisance; their women weren't much better.

And let's not even mention the outsiders, the immigrants, they also didn't say, warm and safe in their lives. The rain fell outside, on the less worthy, in their opinion; they read all the red-top newspapers, they knew the score.

Better them than me, they also didn't say, dunking their biscuits into the cup for just the right amount of time, and the ritual observed, the biscuits eaten, the tea drunk, they went on with their day.

The thing about disease is…it knows no boundaries.

Death visits us all, rich or poor, saint or sinner.

There is no safe place.

The lines in Chief Ben's careworn face hardened. His blue eyes sparked.

"Are you absolutely certain about this, Dorian?" asked the chief.

The selkie nodded.

"Yes, I saw it myself," he replied.

"Was Leah exposed?" asked Chief Ben.

Leah nodded, her mouth drawn tight. She knew enough about the Black Death to be worried, and she was definitely in agreement with Dorian's plan.

"Yes," said Dorian, "We need to get her out of the city immediately."

"You're in luck," said the chief. "Magnus's trial begins tomorrow."

Dorian held his gaze, pensive.

"The three of you wait here," said Chief Ben. "I'll be back with your paperwork in a moment."

14

The three of them silently waited for his return, until Yoo Min spoke.

"Drinking is like eating for lazy people," said Yoo Min, apropos of nothing. "You don't even have to chew."

Yoo Min did this often. She enjoyed making other people uncomfortable, particularly when she was hungry. As a predator she had never quite understood how to get on with other people.

Yoo Min grinned at Leah, trying for a winning smile, but her sharp teeth and horror-movie-wide mouth didn't help. Leah gave her a strange look.

"So," she asked, "What kind of creature are you?"

Yoo Min smiled brightly, only serving to make Leah edge away a bit.

"A gumiho," she said.

Leah backed away a little more, inadvertently. Yoo Min did not seem to notice; she continued to smile, looking slightly unhinged.

"The nine-tailed fox woman?" Leah asked.

"Yes, *sunbae*," Yoo Min confirmed, using the honorific title of *more experienced person*.

"That eats the livers of men?" asked Leah.

"Yes, *sunbae*," Yoo Min said again.

"Dorian," said Leah, turning him around by the shoulder.

"Yes, Leah, what is it?" he asked, his mind elsewhere.

"Dorian," Leah hissed, "Gumiho are *dangerous*. Very dangerous."

Dorian shrugged.

"Well, keep an eye on her then," he said, "She's working *with* us, you know, Miss Bishop."

"That's *Detective* Bishop to you, Earl Grey," said Leah.

Dorian nodded.

"Of course. My apologies, Detective," he said.

Leah turned to look at Yoo Min again, who was still smiling.

"I am very good with knives," said Yoo Min brightly.

"That's...good to know."

Chief Ben turned the corner, papers in hand. He gave a stack to each of them.

"Everything is in order, you can leave today," said Chief Ben. "Stop by the lab and talk to Milo about what you saw with Dylan in that close before you go; we're going to need all hands on deck if there is an outbreak. Milo's our best bet on this one. He's the best forensic pathologist we've ever had, and he specialised in virology."

"Where did he specialise?" asked Leah. "I can't imagine that Glasgow uni would've taken kindly to a man with a tail. Well, maybe not, but he'd have ended up in the Hunterian anatomy collection."

"He didn't attend university here," said Ben.

"Then where?" she pressed, but he wouldn't reply.

"As you say," said Dorian, taking the papers from the chief. "Chief, do we know if it's the human type or…?"

Ben shook his head.

"Not sure which would be worse," he murmured, and Dorian nodded his agreement.

"You want to share with the class?" she asked.

"When we're sure," said Dorian.

"You know, I'm getting tired of being the last one with the information around here," griped Leah. "You guys wanted a human officer, here I am. But you've gotta let me in on what's going on."

"Leah, please trust me, there is a good reason for all of this," said Dorian.

"Yeah? Because it's starting to look kind of sexist. Or species…ist," Leah said.

"I assure you," Ben said, "there are good reasons, but Dorian will fill you in."

Dorian nodded, and they turned to go. Leah stopped.

"Wait, why do we need papers if we're only going to the Highlands?" asked Leah.

"We're going further than the Highlands," he said.

"What is *with* you and all this mysterious crap?!" asked Leah, exasperated.

Dorian favoured her with a little half-smile, and walked out the door.

"Just *once*, I wish you'd answer me straight," muttered Leah, who followed him.

***

"What did you find?" asked Chief Ben.

Yoo Min looked up at him from the computer.

"Stolen passports," she said, "reported at the entry point in Edinburgh, down at the statue of Greyfriars Bobby."

Ben stared at her.

"Hmph," he said, "I suppose I can see that. Enough people believe in the legend of Greyfriars Bobby, it makes sense the wall would be thinner there."

"Yes," Yoo Min confirmed, "and where they find the thin places, and no doors, they push through. People will make a door anywhere. Still. For some reason, there seems to me a brisk trade in stolen passports. I'm not sure if it's humans buying their way into Faerie without realising the price, or if it's Fae themselves trading back and forth. Illegal immigration, either way."

"Stolen?" he asked, "Are the Fae capable of that?"

Yoo Min nodded.

"It doesn't take much," she said, "Our passports are not very difficult; created by a people more obsessed with style than technology. We have much to learn from the humans in that way. I was once skilled at calligraphy. Now I am skilled at forgery. The past is the past, Chief Ben. Forging passports is not difficult. So the question is – why stolen? Not forged?"

Ben raised an eyebrow. She shrugged.

"Gotta make money somehow," she said.

"You're the police!" he said. "Also, I'm your boss, Yoo Min. You should probably not be telling me -"

Yoo Min gave him a long look.

"I think the fact that I have eaten over 70,000 livers of young men should worry you more than my dabbling in forged paperwork," she said, "War is war. That war you won't tell your Detective Bishop about. Someone had to get them out. There was no line, back then, between the Seelie and Unseelie court, as you know. We were all on one side or the other, regardless of our level of monstrosity."

"You knew about the war, all the way over there?" asked Ben.

Yoo Min stared at him, her eyes dark.

"*Everyone* knew," said Yoo Min. "It was *our* world war, so to speak."

A chill descended on the room that had nothing to do with its weather. Ben glanced up to see the sun shining as clouds scudded across the ceiling. Yoo Min just kept staring at him.

The phone rang, startling him. Ben went to pick it up.

"Dorian," he said. "What is it?"

Ben paused.

"What?" he said, "You can't be serious. Nour doesn't usually need help -"

Yoo Min looked at him curiously.

He put the phone down.

"Looks like you have a reprieve from desk work," he said, "Dorian needs you. Apparently Nour-el-ain - she's one of our officers - is fighting some redcaps in the alley behind the off-licence. Dorian has requested your assistance."

Yoo Min smiled, and went to get her coat.

Dorian and Leah were walking to the train station when Yoo Min caught up with them. Dorian's mouth turned down, obviously displeased.

"What brings you here, Yoo Min?" he enquired politely, an edge to his words.

"What are you doing? Are you coming with us?" asked Leah.

"Only to the train station," said Yoo Min, smiling sweetly, "Chief Ben wanted me to get him some coffee."

"Caledonia Interpol is underneath a coffee shop," Leah

pointed out.

"Yes, but he wanted something special," she said.

Dorian rounded on her.

"I'm *going!*" he snapped, "I don't need a chaperone! Besides, Miss Bishop – *Detective* Bishop - would make sure I did as I said. Ben doesn't need to push me; I am going to the trial."

"Chief Ben wants to make sure of that too," said Yoo Min, whose smile was really starting to get on Leah's nerves.

A fireball exploded against the wall above their heads, cutting off the conversation.

"*What in the everloving hell –* " Leah shouted from her crouched position.

There was a beautiful woman walking towards them, as though it was a pleasant afternoon stroll, as she flicked fireballs at a few attackers. She wore a hijab and was taller in her flats than Leah would ever be in high heels.

"What's going on?" asked Leah.

"The redcaps are fighting," said Dorian. "Times of strife, they come out of the woodwork."

"Painted their caps in blood, yeah," said Leah. "I remember."

"They'll do it again, given the chance," said Dorian grimly. "We try to prevent these things. The human world is not going to deal with the suffering well, if the plague takes hold, and the redcaps, like many other creatures, are opportunistic. We try not to allow the opportunity."

He raised a hand in greeting to the woman fighting.

"Good afternoon, Nour-el-ain," said Dorian.

"Hi, Dorian!" chirped the woman, as if she were absolutely thrilled to see him, to be throwing fire in a small alley, and to be alive.

Leah, now that she understood the situation, threw herself into the fight as she saw one of the attackers rise again. Now that she knew the woman was on their side, she'd put her all into it. Or at least her boot, to kerb them on the pavement.

Dorian was momentarily surprised to see Dylan leaning against the stone wall, watching the proceedings. The selkie nodded to the angel, who bowed his head in reply, and they turned their attention to the action.

"Splendid!" Dorian called out, as Leah got in a good punch to the gut, "Oh, good show!"

Dylan hesitated.

"Er," he began, "Do you think we ought to help –"

"No," said Dorian. He watched the fight with the enthusiasm of a sports fan.

"You can join anytime!" called Leah, kicking one of the assailants, but Dorian waved her away.

One of the men got close to Yoo Min, who was also standing and observing the fight. She turned, unsheathed a wicked-looking hand scythe, and eviscerated the man within moments. Covered in blood, she turned back to watch the rest of the fight.

"I think," Dylan said to Leah, clearing his throat and staring at Yoo Min, "I think you're doing all right yourselves."

Nour-el-ain walked over to the other two women as the men were now on the ground, unlikely to move.

"Thanks for the help," she said, "I'm PC Nour-el-ain, but you can call me Nour. I'm a phoenix."

"Detective Inspector Lee Yoo Min," said Yoo Min, "Gumiho."

Nour-el-ain turned to Leah.

"And you are…?" she prompted.

"Detective Inspector Leah Bishop," said Leah, "Human."

This seemed to impress Nour. She clapped her hands in joy.

"Human!" she said, as if she had never seen one before. "Wow, so it's true! Aww, cute!"

Leah narrowed her eyes.

"How come I've never heard of you before?" she asked.

Instead of being insulted, Nour laughed.

"Oh, they never tell us lower levels anything!" she said, "And the sooner you realise the truth of that, the better. There are a lot of us here in Glasgow, officers from all over the world. Some have partners, some work alone. I'm one of the latter."

She turned to Yoo Min.

"That was some incredible work. Welcome to Caledonia Interpol, Yoo Min."

Yoo Min bowed.

"Thank you," she said, and bowed.

Dorian sauntered over to them, a newspaper folded under his arm, as though he was about to congratulate them on a fine sport played on a summer green somewhere outside London. Leah could almost see the glass of Pimm's in his hand.

"Fat lot of good you were, selkie," Leah said, "Basking in the sun."

Dorian closed his eyes and sniffed, choosing to ignore the slight.

"You had it under control," he said. "I wasn't going to get in the way. Besides, my suit was pressed just this morning."

He turned and bowed to Nour.

"Our train is leaving in half an hour, we had best leave," said Dorian, "My compliments on your fighting, Nour-el-ain."

"My compliments on your suit," she returned with a smirk, "Where are you going?"

At this, Dorian's eyes darkened.

"To my brother's trial," he said.

Nour's expression was soft.

"I wish you the best, Dorian Grey," she said, "Do not suffer too much on his behalf."

"It was nice to meet you, Nour," said Yoo Min, taking her leave.

"Yeah, see you around," said Leah, "We could use a few more fighters around here, what with these lazy seals. Wrap them in blubber and they'd sleep for a fortnight."

"Leah..." Dorian warned.

"Yeah, yeah," said Leah, "C'mon, let's go."

Nour-el-ain watched them walk away down the alley.

"I hope we won't need to see each other too soon, Leah Bishop," Nour said, "I truly do."

CHAPTER THREE

Yeah was thrilled to get out into the countryside after so long in the city. Dorian was not similarly moved. The mountains hemmed them close as they travelled through the circuitous countryside, the roads wrapping around the lochs and mountains.

She looked around at the barren and desolate landscape, and thought of her university professors lecturing on the *sublime.* This was the concept of something beautiful *and* terrible, lovely *and* dangerous. The paintings by Landseer were considered sublime – gorgeous, and ominous.

Crunch.

Dorian looked at his partner.

Crunchcrunchcrunchcrunchcrunch

"I *say*, Miss Bishop," he said.

Leah froze, cheddar and onion crisps in her hand. She dropped them back into the bag.

"It's beautiful, isn't it?" she asked, indicating the view out the window.

"If you like this sort of thing," he replied.

"Aren't your people from around here?" she said.

"If you mean the fae, some of them, yes," he said, "Selkies originate further west. But you'll find I have no love for my home either."

"I don't understand that," said Leah, "it's breathtaking."

Dorian just stared out the window.

"What are we doing in the Highlands, Dorian? We are supposed to be watching Glasgow."

"This is where the Council will hold Magnus's trial," said

Dorian.

"What, all the way up here?" asked Leah.

"Yes," he replied. "It's difficult to get the selk to leave Seal-Hame. This was considered a crime the selkies would need to bring to trial, so here we are."

"You said you were afraid," Leah said, "but I've never seen you scared of anything until we arrived in the Highlands. Is there something I don't know?"

"The problem is that the Guardians are all that guards the city from the monsters and supernaturals who come down from the Highlands," said Dorian, "and it is from that direction that we have the most to fear. We have always known this. Those who wanted to stay with the old ways stayed in the mountains. Those who wanted to move forward with the times moved to Glasgow, Edinburgh, Aberdeen – or even went over the seas, like other immigrants. The sun never set on the British Empire, and so many monsters moved away. This was in fact the start of the Interpol – not of the police, but of the international nature of the force. Much like your people now have world summits, diplomats, and expats – so does every nation of monster and mythological creature."

"Is it difficult to get a monster passport?" asked Leah.

"About the same as it is to get a human one," said Dorian, "but monsters don't care a fig about immigration. The world is ours. The entire world. It was ours before humans were here and will be ours after you go. We do not feel threatened by each other in the same way humans do – but we will stop our own from the wholesale harvest of human life."

"Okay," said Leah. "But you and Ben – you wanted me out of the city because you think I'm infected, right?"

Dorian pursed his lips.

"We don't know for certain," said Dorian. "I thought it prudent to get out out and away from the human population just in case."

Leah examined her fingers, which were covered in crisp dust.

"They look okay to me," she said.

"It can take time, Leah," said Dorian sternly.

"Well, either way, it's good to get out of the city," she said. "It's like a mini holiday!"

"Indeed," said Dorian, but concern was written on his pale features.

The train stopped with a quiet sigh, that much louder because their destination was one of the most remote train stops in the Highlands. Humans weren't aware of the reasons for the development and placement of Altnabreac Station, but the Fae knew all too well.

As they stood together on the platform, Leah watched the train go, and the desolate mountains seemed to crowd in on her and Dorian.

Dorian began to walk across the moor, silently, and Leah followed. The mist began to descend as they approached the mountains on the opposite side of the moor, and wrapped itself around them as they began to ascend. Leah began to lose sight of Dorian, as he picked his way up the mountain with an air of etiquette that felt out of place in this mountainous terrain. Soon, his black-clad back disappeared and she could see nothing more than mist.

"Dorian?" called Leah, quietly.

She stood on the side of the mountain, stock-still. The mist was a shawl around her shoulders, obscuring her view.

"If I don't end up getting eaten by a monster, I'm going to fall to my death," she muttered, afraid to shout for Dorian in case it marked her location. Monsters in the quiet brooding Highlands, with its eerie silence, were a much different experience than when they made you coffee and asked about your day.

"Here," murmured Dorian, briefly touching her; she nearly jumped out of her skin.

"Dorian Grey!" she snarled, "Don't do that. You scared the crap out of me."

"Look," he said, nodding in the direction of the glen below.

Leah stared into the white and was about to ask him what

he meant when the mist cleared enough for her to see strange shapes, weird creatures with long, bonelike arms.

Their greyish-white forms seemed as though they were part of the landscape, until she saw them walking.

"Those are the Attendants," Dorian said. Leah looked at him, puzzled.

"The primary Guardian's servants," he explained, "They never leave Glasgow. Ever. They know better. Look what happened when Aonghas decided to have a few drinks in Dublin."

"Maybe ... it wasn't Aonghas's fault after all," Leah whispered back. "What's going on here, Dorian?"

He shook his head.

"I really don't know," he replied. "Every creature has their home-place. For me, and for Magnus, that's Islay, the land above Seal-Hame. For Aonghas, it's Glasgow, and was Glasgow back when it could accurately be called 'the dear green place'. We are not creatures that move."

"And yet Yoo Min is here," Leah said.

"The necessities of an international police force," said Dorian.

She then stood up, and motioned for Dorian to follow. They wound their way down the mountain and into the darkness of the caves below.

***

Leah couldn't see. It was so dark in the cave that the only visible light was the small pinpoint from the entrance. She kept stumbling and swearing under her breath.

"Take this," said Dorian's voice at her elbow, handing her one end of a rope.

"You mean you can see down here?" she asked.

"Yes," he replied.

He turned to her, and she wasn't as surprised as she once would have been to see that his eyes were a luminescent blue, like the phosphorescent waters in the southern oceans.

They continued into the blackness. Leah shut her eyes and

26

opened them. It made no difference.

"You're lucky I trust you," she said.

"You can buy me a fish when we're done," Dorian's voice floated back to her from somewhere in the distance.

"Don't you vanish on me, Dorian Grey," she said.

"Don't worry, Leah," he said, his voice now near her elbow. "Come over here."

He tugged on the rope and she followed. A dull light was visible and as her eyes adjusted she saw that they were on a ledge, overlooking a large interior room in the belly of the cave. Dorian lay flat on his stomach and indicated she do the same.

They looked down into the cavernous room. In the time it had taken them to reach this part of the cave, the Attendants had moved into the interior. Behind them, a beautiful waterfall cascaded down into the cave. Dorian shook his head. He stood up and backed away, and Leah stood to join him.

"What is it?" she asked.

"I don't know what's going on here," he said, "but I think I know someone who might."

As the mist of the waterfall cleared, Leah saw the ugliest face she had ever encountered. *It's an urisk,* said the educated part of her mind; *run run run run,* said her lizard brain. She had turned before realising what she was doing, when Dorian gripped her arm.

His hold on her was strong, like a steel vise.

She looked at his hand, and then at his pale, aristocratic features, as though she had never seen him before.

"*Holy –*" she began, but the creature was in front of them, and Dorian let her go. The encounter had been so brief, she could almost convince herself she'd imagined it.

Almost.

"*Dorian!*" the blue-grey thing was shouting, "*Dorian Grey!* I never thought I'd see you again!!!"

"My apologies in advance, Miss Bishop," Dorian murmured, "he can be a bit…extreme."

He turned his attention to the monster.

"Is it really you, Gregoire?"

The urisk, Gregoire was crying real tears, sobbing loudly, as he threw himself into Dorian's arms, nearly knocking him over. Dorian gently extracted himself from Gregoire's embrace, and turned his attention to Leah.

"May I present Detective Inspector Leah Bishop," said Dorian.

Gregoire's eyes went wide and shining with adoration.

"Is she…is she a *human?*" he asked breathlessly.

The edges of Dorian's mouth quirked up in something like a smile.

"Yes," he said.

Gregoire's joy could not be contained. He bowed to the ground, and then enthusiastically shook Leah's hand until it was almost about to fall off.

"Gregoire, Miss Bishop. I would be just absolutely delighted if you would join me for a cup of tea."

Leah was lost for words.

From the side of his mouth, Gregoire asked Dorian, "Too much?"

Leah was startled by the interior of Gregoire's cave. It looked exactly like her grandmother's house would have, if she had been somewhat insane. Tartan tat everywhere, a fireplace with peat burning, terrible wallpaper with too many tiny deer on it – Leah had never been anywhere quite so Scottish. There were squares of tablet on the table, with biscuits, next to little embroidered stitchings of Scottie dogs.

The monster had a tea cosy.

"Sit down here, my lady," said Gregoire, "This is a soft seat I bought especially for humans! It is very soft and comfortable; the shopkeeper assured me that humans really enjoy these seats."

Leah looked doubtfully at the La-Z-Boy, but sat down anyway. This brought a fresh flood of tears from Gregoire and a beatific expression of joy she could not help but smile at. He pushed a cup of tea into her hands and then sat directly in front of her, with his elbows on his knees and his chin in his hands, staring at her and sighing.

Leah turned towards Dorian to improve the view.

"Gregoire is an urisk," said Dorian, grinning, "I have known him for centuries."

"Yes, Dorian," Gregoire said gently, "why have you stayed away for so long?"

"I was Taken," said Dorian, "and then, I thought you were dead."

"Ah, true," said Gregoire, "there were those reports – what a time that was! What a warrior you were. Love seems to suit you well. Congratulations on being Taken, I did not know."

"Thank you," said Dorian.

"Dorian," said Leah, and Gregoire turned attentively to her again, "shouldn't you tell him that she –"

"Oh, of course she must have passed on by now," said Gregoire, hand-waving it away, "but as you know, the great Shakespeare said – better to have loved and lost."

"Not sure I agree," said Leah into her teacup.

"Dorian, is this human *unhappy?!*" demanded Gregoire, "Is it heartbroken?"

"I like to think we're fixing that," said Dorian.

"Poor human!!" cried Gregoire, who suddenly scooped Leah up and cuddled her, "You are always welcome here!"

"Leah is a she," said Dorian, "and a Detective Inspector, you ought to put her down. She bites."

Gregoire looked down at the woman he had crushed in his arms. He released her into the chair.

"Oh, I am sorry," said Gregoire, "we get so few humans here, my lady."

Dorian was clearly amused by their interactions, as Gregoire stared adoringly at Leah. Leah cleared her throat.

"Dorian, can I have a word?" she said. Dorian nodded.

She led him outside, where the night had fallen soft and warm on the shoulders of the mountains.

They stood by the waterfall, where the noise of the water plunging into the stream below would cover their words.

"Explain," she said, arms crossed.

Dorian nodded and smiled.

"I am sorry, Leah," he said. "It's been a long time since I've seen him, and he does so love humans."

"The urisks are waterfall guardians, right?" she asked.

"Yes," said Dorian, "and they absolutely worship and adore humans. Unfortunately, I think only the Nuckelavee rival them in ugliness. The people of the Highlands learned very quickly to run from anything that seemed supernatural – fair or foul. The urisk is not only a guardian of the waterfall, he is also the most faithful soldier the human side could possibly have. This is a problem, because while any urisk will run toward a human in delight, humans will always run away from them. Therefore, many of them are extremely lonely, always hoping to meet humans and never getting the chance. Gregoire and I are friends from a long time back. I think he likes selkies because we are as close to being human as supernaturals can get."

"Yes, he mentioned that you knew each other 'back then'," said Leah, "Back when?"

"I think we met centuries before," said Dorian, "but he is referring to the Fae Wars."

"The what?" asked Leah.

Dorian leaned against the rocks.

"You remember when Chief Ben told you that even faeries have drug problems?" he asked, and she nodded.

"Those are leftovers from the Fae Wars," he said, "Centuries ago, a drug was discovered that worked on all the Fae. It made them feel mortal – the same way that some of your drugs make users feel immortal. Eventually we found out that it was highly addictive, and fatal."

"You never mentioned this before," said Leah.

"It's ancient history," said Dorian, "fun for reminiscing, but not something we would like to see again."

"What happened?" asked Leah.

"It turned out that the drug had an unexpected side effect," said Dorian. "Humans died very quickly from exposure to it, in a way that mimics the Black Plague. There were factions of the Fae that wanted to continue using, and other factions that felt it was irresponsible for Fae and human alike. We are complementary creatures in many ways – if the human race died off there would no longer be food for vampires, or humans for the seal-people to love. The war lasted for an age, and we didn't think it would ever end."

"But it's over now?" asked Leah.

"Yes," Dorian replied, "Caledonia Interpol was instrumental in taking care of the problem, but not without repercussions. And the drug still exists, although most Fae are not foolish enough to try it because they already know the outcome. However, much like humans, that doesn't stop everyone."

"You'd mentioned the monsters who preferred the Fae to be the only creatures around," said Leah. "Did that happen because of the war?"

"No," said Dorian, "it predated the war by thousands of years. The supernatural creatures that wanted to continue to destroy humankind, and those of us that wished to preserve it, had our falling out a very long prior to the start of the Fae Wars. However, it is one example of how history repeats itself, in a way. Back in those days, it was mostly about jealousy and who had the right to exist, because we were here first. The Wars were more about addicts wanting to continue to have a right to their addiction. Some aspects are the same, but the addicts were not driven by any kind of moral justice. They only wanted to continue to use the drug."

"Even though it would kill them too, in the end?" asked Leah.

"Yes," said Dorian. "Humans have the same compunction, in a way."

Thinking of the addicts she had met in her own life, Leah nodded. She also thought of her own interest in alcohol. Addiction was a monster of its own.

Gregoire put his head outside the cave again.

"You aren't going to keep Leah all to yourself, are you, Dorian?" he asked. He looked at her.

"I have made something called 'a Sunday roast'. I have been told humans like this. Would you like to join me, Detective Inspector Leah Bishop?"

***

A few hours later, they were climbing back up the scree to the hill.

"What was in that Sunday roast?" asked Leah, waving to Gregoire, who was standing beside his waterfall waving excitedly.

"I think it was just a roast, Leah," said Dorian, "Something a supernatural learns very early on is that beautiful things are often the evil things. Ugly creatures like Gregoire are often of good heart. It's unlikely he'd serve anything dangerous to us."

"That doesn't say much for the selkies," she said. The pained look that crossed his face for a moment told Leah it was Magnus Dorian was thinking of, and she fell silent.

They emerged onto the road side and walked together to a lonely train station, the loneliest in the Highlands.

"So, what next?" asked Leah.

"I think we need to find a village and stay there," Dorian said, "I'm not entirely convinced that we have run into a dead end. I think that Gregoire knows something. He's been out of the army so long, and away from the fighting, that I can well imagine he does not want to get involved again."

The train eventually arrived, as the dawn wreathed the mountains in sun breaking through the towering clouds. Leah faced the direction the train was going, and looked out at the landscape. Beautiful as it was, she wondered what would come of them if the train broke down in such a desolate area. The mountains hemmed them in, covered in snow, and the early morning fog crept through the glens.

"I wouldn't think about it," Dorian said, as if she'd spoken. "Especially not in winter."

"Ugh, it's so *creepy* when you do that," she said, but there was no force behind it. "We do live in a modern age, Dorian. I'm sure we'd be all right."

"It is not the modern age that worries me," he said, visibly uncomfortable as he looked out the window. "I will feel better when I am back in the city."

Leah was surprised to see him this way.

"Are you...*scared*, Dorian?" she asked, her eyes widening.

He nodded.

CHAPTER FOUR

The train stopped and Dorian indicated they needed to get out. Leah followed him, stopping at a tiny store to buy a packet of McCoy's Cheddar and Onion crisps and some Irn-Bru.

"Hungry?" asked Dorian mildly.

"Starving," she said. "Do you think this place has food?"

A smile ghosted across Dorian's features.

"Almost certain of it," he replied.

The long twilight of a Scottish summer evening lit their way to a whitewashed hotel. The ocean lay beyond it, blue and still.

"*The Angels' Share*," Leah read the hotel's sign aloud. "This isn't going to be like *American Werewolf in London*, is it?"

"Oh no," said Dorian, "Scotland only has wulvers."

"Right," said Leah. "Leaving fish on windowsills for the poor. Always seemed odd that the only werewolf in Scotland was a creature whose only activity was giving food to poor people."

"People were starving," said Dorian. "They needed something to believe."

"Strange," she said. "Seems like the most terrifying monsters are the kindest."

"There is no such common rule," he said. "It depends on the monster. Some ugly, some beautiful, some plain."

"Something about not judging a book by its cover," said Leah.

"Oh no," said Dorian. "You see, we're *all monsters*. That's what you have to remember, above all other things."

They pushed the door open and went inside.

The hotel was the standard, ancient structure found in the Highlands; small and white, with a wooden interior, tartan carpeting meeting white walls. Embers glowed in the grating of a rough stone fireplace. A border collie slept beside it, and the place was filled with the smoky scent of peat.

Inside the bar, a few patrons sat nursing drinks or playing darts. The tables were wooden, the floor made of the same worn tartan carpet, and the walls and bar were of rich, dark wood.

Leah was pleased to see a vast whisky selection, and even more pleased with the bartender.

He was what dreams of Scotland are made of.

The man was tall, with black hair that fell across his forehead and curled around his ears. His high cheekbones were dusted with a natural rose. He had fiery, strange whisky-coloured eyes. The shirtsleeves of his white button-down were rolled up to the elbow, exposing muscular forearms. His strong jawline, broad shoulders, and effortless air of insouciant confidence were an amalgam of every Scottish fantasy. He saw Dorian and smiled broadly.

"Well. Dorian Grey," said the bartender, "I didn't think I would ever see you around here again."

He stepped out from behind the bar and Leah was able to fully appreciate the view. He shook Dorian's hand.

"Who's your pretty friend? Don't tell me you've sworn off all that angst and Taken nonsense," said the man, his smouldering eyes levelled at Leah.

"Never," said Dorian. "This is my partner, Detective Inspector Leah Bishop."

"Pleased to meet you," he said, canting his head with a sly grin. "I'm Robert Burns."

Leah did not realise her mouth was open til Dorian jostled her.

"Steady there, Leah," he said. "This one's taken."

"May I present Detective Inspector Leah Bishop," said Dorian, bowing to the stranger, "Leah, may I present Robert Burns, Scottish national poet and the proprietor of this fine establishment."

A thousand images, hundreds of paintings, of poems, of stories went through her mind like a wind whirling autumn leaves. She thought of moments in his life, his songs, his words, and she stared at the man standing before her. His lazy grin, the merry, suggestive look in his strange, wide eyes, the man's obvious self-assurance, his lofty carriage...it must be him.

"You can close your mouth now, Leah," whispered Dorian. Leah shut her mouth with a snap.

"*This is **the** Robert Burns?*" she whispered back, as if he wasn't standing right in front of her.

Robert smiled.

"There are, after all, so many," he said.

"I once read," she said, "that the body – *your* body – was exhumed, and you were in perfect condition, as if you were still alive –"

"And that someone touched my cheek with a finger, and I collapsed into dust?" smiled Robert. "Yes, I was there. Fortunately, we can reconstruct from anything."

"Careful there, Leah," said Dorian. "This one's taken."

"Taken?" she asked. "*Taken?* He's a selkie?"

Robert laughed, and then offered Leah a half-smile that told her exactly why he had the reputation he did.

"No," he said. "I'm a vampire."

"Robert Burns is a vampire?" asked Leah, her eyes goggled. "Whisky, please, Bruichladdich, now."

Robert Burns winked at her and went to get a glass. Dorian put his hand under her elbow.

They sat down. Or rather, Dorian primly took his seat and Leah collapsed in a heavy whuff across from him.

Dorian opened the menu, all Victorian nonchalance.

Leah stared at him.

"*Dorian!!!*" she hissed.

"Yes, Miss Bishop? The Loch Fyne oysters are good, but maybe fish..." he mused.

"*Dorian Grey, put that menu down right now,*" Leah said. Dorian put down the menu.

"Yes?" he asked.

"***Robert Burns,*** *Dorian, and he's a* ***bartender*** *in some no-where place in the Highlands?! And you didn't tell me in advance?*" Leah hissed.

"He's an excellent cook as well," said Dorian, "as to *some no-where place*, I'm not sure that is true. I recommend the fish, I really do."

"You always recommend the fish," she said, exasperated. "What do you mean, it's not some nowhere place?"

"Well, you know how Magnus will be tried by the faerie tribunal?" asked Dorian.

"Yes?" asked Leah.

"You didn't expect that was a place in *your world*, did you?" he asked.

"So this is –"

Dorian nodded.

"The entrance to Faerie."

"I might faint," she said, clearly not about to do anything of the sort. "The things you never tell me. You could have warned me!"

"And what would be the fun in that?" asked Dorian. "Robert has always been here, will always be here. He's as much a part of Scotland as Ben Cruachan. He is immortal, like Desdemona, and like myself."

Robert set down two glasses of whisky on the table and took the chair next to Leah.

"Truly immortal...the immortal bard. Take that, Shakespeare," he said. "Nothing can kill me. Believe me, I've tried. I just keep coming back."

"As do we all," said Dorian ruefully.

"It must have been very difficult to have a war," said Leah. "If nobody died, I mean."

Robert and Dorian exchanged glances.

"There is always a way," he said. "Have you read the Cask of Amontillado?"

"Yes, of course," said Leah, "Oh."

"Poe's story of Fortunato and his friend," Dorian said. "Appropriate. Yes. He's bricked into a wall and left to die there."

"You people don't mess around," said Leah, and Dorian nodded.

Robert touched the whisky to his lips. Leah watched, fascinated, as he ran his tongue out to catch the droplets.

Dorian nudged her foot under the table. Apparently Robert was speaking. She shook herself out of some interesting daydreams.

"Punishments, for the Fae, tend to be very Greek," he was saying, "Sisyphus rolling the boulder up the hill, Tantalus stretching out his hand for the grapes always just out of his reach, that sort of thing."

"There is death, and there is worse than death," said Dorian, "and *worse than death* is often the fate of the fae."

"But if Magnus is given the death sentence, how would that be carried out?" asked Leah.

"The severity of his crimes may call for it," said Dorian, "and although we survive much, we cannot endure everything."

Leah looked at Dorian. His face was impassive.

The three of them sat in silence, listening to the crackle of the fire. Leah reached down to pet the Border collie, who had since woken up and padded over, nudging her hand with its nose.

"What's his name?" asked Leah.

"Dileas," said Robert. "They're all named that up here."

"What, every dog has the same name?" she asked.

"Scottish law. The minute you cross the Highland border you're issued with a Border collie named Dileas," he said, merriment in his eyes.

"Well, I haven't received mine," she said, petting Dileas.

"City folk don't get one," said Robert. "You only get the dog if you're brave enough to relocate to the Highlands."

Dorian coughed and shot Leah a look.

"What?" she asked.

"If you're done flirting," said Dorian.

"We were having a conversation!" she protested.

"His eyes are up there," said Dorian drily.

"He's insufferable, you know," Leah confided in Robert.

"I know," said Robert. "And you don't know the half of it. Things were different once."

Before Leah had a chance to ask what he meant, Dorian had resumed speaking, voice tinged with irritation.

"I see you've made a friend," said Dorian.

"Yeah," said Leah. "Maybe I should get a pet."

Dileas had decided to fall asleep with his head in her lap. The room was warm, the wind whistled against the panes of glass, and the fire crackled on as she drained her whisky. Robert went to fetch the bottle, and a thought crossed Leah's mind, leaving her grinning.

"So tell me," she said, as Robert poured whisky into her glass and set the bottle down on the table, "did you really have sixteen illegitimate children?"

Robert grinned again. His smile could light up the darkness.

"Sixteen! Is that what the number is now?" he said. "And no, it was twelve in total, although many died in childhood, more's the pity. The times, you know. Some of them were legitimate. In fact, many of them have been great successes! I kept an eye on the exploits of my children, and their children's children, with great interest. Unfortunately, not a word of poetry in any of them!"

"Must have been a one-time thing," said Leah, sipping her whisky, relishing the way the peat-smoke flavour faded away on her tongue. "Did you know you have over 900 direct descendants?"

Robert paled, if such a thing were possible.

"I *what*?!"

"Yeah," said Leah offhandedly. "It's more a surprise if someone in Scotland *isn't* related to you than if they are. Well done. I suppose you've kept the Scottish race alive."

Robert did not reply, but downed his whisky and poured the next one to the rim of his glass.

***

Gregoire put the kettle on the fire, humming to himself. He had purchased some candy through one of his suppliers, and hoped that Miss Bishop would return to partake of it with him. She was the first human in centuries that had not run away screaming from him, but he knew that was partly Dorian's influence. He smiled to himself and shook his head. *Dorian.* He remembered what the man used to be like. He had never met the brother but he was fairly certain all Untaken selkies behaved the same way.

A loud, keening wail sounded outside in the darkness. Gregoire stood still.

The sound came again.

Gregoire crept outside, past his waterfall, and leaned out to look into the valley below.

"I thought so," he sighed, dismay etching itself upon his horrible features. "No wonder they were all the way up here, asking questions. It has returned."

The wind whipped the trees into a frenzy, their branches scratching and spidering against the window in the darkness. Everyone slept through this because it was a normal night in Scotland.

Until it wasn't.

***

Leah sat bolt upright in bed and instantly regretted it, her hangover and the freezing room vying for her attention. She split the difference, grabbing the duvet and curling it around her, as she rescued the hot water bottle where it had fallen on the floor.

A roar shook the windows, rattling the panes of the ancient hotel that had not yet heard of double glazing or insulation. She opened the window and looked out into the darkness. There was mist on the ground and a soft eldritch light glowing. She heard the sound again...a keening, wailing sound. Her blood ran cold.

She saw a formless shape move suddenly in the fog, long black claws drawing shadows across the ground. She leaned out the window, trying to catch another glimpse, but all she could see were the white clouds rolling across the earth.

Still, she knew what she had seen.

"Get a grip, Bishop," she said to herself. "You work with monsters. You're safe, and you've seen weirder."

She looked at the duvet and hot water bottle, her heart filled with regret.

"Are you going out there? Yes, you are."

She threw off the duvet, gasping at the cold air even though it was a summer night.

She dressed quickly, and went across the hall to Dorian's bedroom. She knocked at the door, and after a moment, it opened.

Dorian stood there, looking radiant and perfect in a smoking jacket, not a jet-black strand of hair out of place.

"Don't you sleep?" she asked.

"I was sleeping," he said.

"...Huh. The selkie power of perfect hair," Leah snorted. "Anyway, I saw something outside in the fog. It was making a strange noise. Could be nothing."

Dorian gave her a look, steel behind the soft brown of his eyes.

"It's never nothing, Leah," he said. "Give me a moment to change into something more appropriate."

"If you come out here wearing some kind of Sherlock Holmes outfit, I swear to God," muttered Leah, but she shut the door.

The door closed softly, and Leah was alone in the hallway. She decided to use the bathroom, because who knew how long a selkie would take to get ready to his satisfaction after being woken up in the middle of the night.

A voice spoke directly into her ear.

He thrusts his fists against the posts
and still insists he sees the ghosts...
He thrusts his fists against the posts
and still insists he sees the ghosts...

The voice was as loud as if there was someone in the hallway. Leah turned, slowly.

"Hello?" she asked. "Is someone here?"

There was no response.

A little discomfited, she went to use the bathroom.

As she washed her hands, she looked up into the mirror.

A woman was standing behind her.

She whipped around. The room was empty.

Tap.

Tap. Tap.

Slowly, she turned toward the window. *I'm on the fourth floor*, she thought.

There was nothing there.

Tap.

Tap. Tap.

Tap. Tap. Tap.

She wheeled slowly around as she realised where the sound was coming from.

TAP. TAP. TAP.

The mirror. The sound was coming from the mirror.

She slammed her hand into the light switch and the room flooded with yellow-white.

In the mirror was a beautiful woman with dark hair, blood trickling from the edge of her mouth.

Leah gasped and whirled around, but there was no one there. She turned back and the mirror was also empty.

Shit.

She backed out of the bathroom and opened the hallway door. All was darkness there as well, except for the dull emergency light from the exit.

Back down the darkened hallway to Dorian's bedroom, she

couldn't shake the feeling that she really shouldn't turn around.

"*Dorian,*" she tried, but her throat was dry and no sound came out. She edged towards his door.

"**Dorian,**" she managed to hiss. Her hands found the doorknob. She turned it and fell inside.

Dorian turned from a large vanity where he had been straightening his jacket in the mirror. Startled, he went to her.

"Leah?" he asked. "What's wrong?!"

"A ghost," she said. "There's a ghost, I saw it."

Dorian raised an eyebrow.

"I saw a woman's face in the mirror," she said, and before Dorian could point out the obvious, "Not me! I mean, a different woman."

"Ghosts," said Dorian, "Ugh, they are such a waste of time, you can't get any sleep. Wonderful."

"So you've seen ghosts before?" she asked.

"Oh, yes. Some of my best friends are ghosts," Dorian replied.

"You have other friends?" asked Leah, startled.

Dorian gave her a Look.

"Not like that!" Leah said, "I just meant I've never seen you with any."

"Well, Miss Bishop," said Dorian, "I could say the same for you."

"That's not the same!" she said, "I just moved back to Glasgow! You've been there since the French Revolution!"

"Not true," he said, "I've only been in Glasgow since the turn of the century."

"Okay, but the war..."

"I will tell you the story later, but now, let's find out what's outside – if it hasn't left already."

They went down the stairs and opened the door. The mist was thick, roiling around the hotel and blanking out the mountainous landscape.

"Don't get too far," said Leah, "I don't know if we're going to find anything in this."

Dorian's eyes glowed.

"Follow me," he said.

She walked into the mist.

"Dorian?" she said. He had vanished.

And the keening cry sounded again, very close.

As she peered through the mist, she suddenly backed up and fell over. A monster towered over her. A real monster, not like Dorian or Ben or Milo – a fleshless man, with lidless eyes yellow with a strange light, and long arms at the end of which were claws. He rode a fleshless horse, and both horse and man had scything teeth like an anglerfish.

She made a strange noise in her throat. She knew what it was, but she had never realised the nightmare of its reality.

The mist circled around them, and hid the Nuckelavee from sight once again, as it leaned its head back, opened the needle-teeth, and made the same keening wail. It acted as if it had not seen her.

"Leah?" said a voice beside her shoulder. She hit Dorian on the arm.

"Where were you?" she said.

"What do you mean? I was right here," he replied.

"Liar," she said. "There's a Nuckelavee here. It was maybe three steps from me!"

"I thought as much," said Dorian, "I heard its cry, just now."

"So, what should we do?" she asked. "Do we arrest it? How?"

"I'm not sure it's done anything illegal," he said.

"That monster? I'm pretty sure it has!" she said.

"Looks aren't everything," he said. "One of the Guardians of Glasgow is a Nuckelavee."

"So you think this one might be the missing Guardian?" she asked. "What's the big deal, anyway? A lot of Glasgow monsters are here; seems like a weird place for a holiday, and strange timing."

"A lot of monsters want to see Magnus brought to justice," Dorian said.

"Including you?" she asked.

His mouth set, he nodded.

They walked down the narrow stairs of the hotel and went into the pub. Robert was behind the bar, cleaning up. He saw them enter, and threw a white towel over his shoulder, leaning against the bar in a way that told Leah exactly what he'd be like if she pushed him up against the counter and –

"Did you hear that?" asked Dorian.

"Yes," Robert said, and turned to take an old shotgun off the wall. Very old. The folklorist in Leah was curious, and as he passed by her, the nickel plate on the gun winked in the low light.

For RB. From Des.

She narrowed her eyes. *Des*? It had to be a coincidence. Not Desdemona, the grumpy cabaret vampire in Glasgow? It couldn't be.

They walked outside into the mist and silence of a Highland night. It was nearly 3 am; the sun would be up soon, chasing the fog away until the shadows of the mountains brought the chill and darkness again in the early afternoon. There was not much light up here in the mountains, thought Leah. She looked at Robert's white face, the slight rosy blush to his cheeks, the innocence that still played across his features, and his sharpened teeth, and she wondered who he was saving himself for. He could be living it up in Glasgow, Edinburgh – hell, even outside of Scotland, if he wanted – but it was clear to her that he'd chosen this darkness for some reason.

The loud scream and sudden appearance of the Nuckelavee would not have startled Leah as much as it did if she hadn't been distracted by Robert Burns, but as it was, she headbutted it in its horselike face, like any good Glasgow girl would do. It went down heavily, both horse and fused rider, with a whimper, and rolled over, unconscious.

The Nuckelavee, one of the greatest horrors Scotland had to offer, was a skinless horse-and-rider, with scything teeth in both the jaws of the horse and the human, which had long arms with wicked claws that dragged along the ground. Now, silent in its sleep, it was horrifying but sad somehow, as if its legend had died along with it.

Dorian and Robert exchanged a glance. Robert looked down at his unused rifle and back at the Nuckelavee. Dorian leaned down and examined the still form of the monster.

"Do you see this, Robert?" asked Dorian.

He turned the arm of the Nuckelavee over, pointing at several pockmarks at the monster's elbow, a contrasting dark blue to the red of its fleshless body. Robert nodded and sighed.

"Not all that appears evil is evil," Robert said to Leah. "Nuckelavee are normally cruel and vicious monsters. Not this one. This is the missing Guardian of your city. He must have returned to the Highlands, in the hallucinations near the end."

"Near the end of what?" asked Leah. Robert's delicate eyebrows arched.

"The end of his life," said Robert. "It was an addict, Leah."

"An addict? Addicted to what?" she asked. This time, Robert didn't answer, staring down at the body.

"I did not think we would see fae opium again," Dorian sighed.

"Is that the drug you were talking about before? Either of you want to fill me in?" asked Leah. "I thought that the Guardian was killed, back during Sebastian's murder spree."

The Nuckelavee took a last, shuddering breath, and expired.

"It is truly dead, now," said Robert. "But it died a living death a long time ago. You see?"

"The moment it was incapable of caretaking, Dylan was called," Dorian explained.

"Why would someone want them dead anyway?" Leah asked, "Guardians are replaced."

"Yes, but a new and inexperienced one is different than an older Guardian," Robert explained.

A loud, keening wail echoed through the glen. They looked at each other.

"What was that?" asked Leah. "The Nuckelavee is dead!"

Robert looked at Dorian, and then shouldered the rifle.

"Get inside now," he growled. "Get behind me."

Dorian and Leah broke into a run, slamming into the hotel's red front door and struggling with the latch before throwing the door open and all but falling inside. Robert backed away as quickly as he could, the sound of great hoofbeats in the distance getting closer, and something clawing the ground, throwing up great clods of dirt.

Robert edged sideways into the doorway, kicking the door shut just as something huge thundered into it, shaking the entire building to its very beams. Robert shot the lock home, and then backed away, shouldering the gun again and sighting down the barrel. He cocked the lever-action rifle, breathing heavily, his eyes sparked red with fear.

The thing slammed against the side of the hotel again and again. Then the sound of some great animal snuffling at the door could be heard, and at the windows Leah and Dorian wisely stayed away from, their backs against the wall.

The thing made a sighing sound, and its hoofbeats could be heard, receding away down the glen. There was not much darkness left in the night, it being the height of summer, and Robert let out a breath as he lowered the gun. His entire body relaxed. He stared at the floor, exhausted, collecting himself.

After a moment, he went back into the bar and put the rifle back on its hooks, touching it with a strange reverence Leah found curious before he turned away. He then went to the bar and set a bottle of whisky on the counter next to three glasses.

"We should be safe inside tonight," he said, a tremor in his voice. The whisky bottle chattered against the glass as he poured. "I think we need this. There's not a day I've been that frightened since I wrote Tam o'Shanter."

Leah studied him, confused. If he were truly immortal, as he claimed, what could be worrying him? Surely he could not care so much about a human he just met, or even Dorian. She sensed that he had some particular interest in self-preservation, and again wondered why.

CHAPTER FIVE

CALEDONIA INTERPOL

hief Ben hazarded a look outside, as he climbed the ivy-covered staircase and walked out of Interpol for his cigarette. The sight that met his eyes unnerved him, as he cupped his hands around his lighter and inhaled deeply.

Glasgow was empty, the city streets bare of people. A few stragglers walked past hurriedly, but the streets held the quiet of death. Fear was a strange thing for humans, a creeping terror or a violent one, but these were the kinds of things none of the Fae could do anything about. Disease was a mystery human doctors had to solve.

Ben breathed out, watching the smoke dissipate in the sunrise. The water of the Clyde danced in the sunlight, just as it always had and probably always would. The giant bowed his head in the face of things they couldn't change, even with all their powers. He hoped, as he always did, that they wouldn't find themselves alone after all, the inheritors of the earth after the human race hand vanished.

This was the trouble, after all, with immortality. Ben put out his cigarette and placed his palm against the red sandstone, the silence of the city ringing out around him until he could close the door to the relative peace of the staircase and the strange fae creatures tittering in the ivy, watching him with their strange alien eyes.

THE ANGEL'S SHARE
SCOTTISH HIGHLANDS

Leah sipped the whisky, the peat-smoke flavour warming her. Robert pushed the coals around in the grate of the fire. Dorian snoozed against the wall, his posture perfect even in slumber.

"You did write a lot about the supernatural," she said, to encourage conversation. She was a detective, and her curiosity had been piqued.

Robert quirked a smile and half-laughed. Leah was momentarily captivated. *He's so fuckin' hot*, she thought. *Yes, and that's exactly how all those other women got in trouble with him*, she reprimanded herself.

"Little did I know that I would become one of them," Robert was saying. "That was a surprise. I can't say I regret it."

Leah shook herself. The slight action wakened Dorian from his nap, although he had apparently been following the conversation.

"Some of us do not get a choice in the matter," said Dorian. "What do you think that was, Robert? There is something going on here and I can't put my finger on it."

"You're the detective," said Robert. "Ever since we last met."

"Yes," smiled Dorian. "I remember. That was quite a night."

Leah could tell her questions weren't going to be answered that night. The three of them sat in the pub, warmed by the fire in the hearth. It was quiet and calm, as usual; it was difficult to believe they had just been chased by a monster.

Leah yawned widely.

"I don't know about the two of you, but I'm beat," said Leah. "I'm off to bed."

Robert nodded.

"Let me know if you need anything," he said, "I'll keep watch tonight."

Dorian stood, smoothing out his coat. He hid a yawn behind one porcelain-perfect hand.

"Thank you, Robert," he said, bowing. "We'll see you in the morning."

Alone in the bar, Robert Burns turned and touched the gun on the wall with something like a lover's caress. He gazed at the inscription, running a finger softly around it, his strange whisky eyes all firelight and sorrow.

"What price, these mortal souls?" he murmured. "Mine for yours. Forever."

***

Leah paced back and forth in her room, grinning to herself.

"Robert Burns," she said, out loud, because she still couldn't quite believe it.

She remembered her university days, where she'd learned about his life and poetry. She'd read that he was handsome, of course, and that many women had been a part of his life despite his somewhat assholish behaviour. She'd frequently wondered why, as he didn't seem all that good-looking based on the paintings, so they weren't much to go on. Men that behaved the way he did weren't always so lucky in love. *Treat 'em mean, keep 'em keen*, she had told herself back then.

But now, seeing him in flesh and blood, there was something about his personal beauty that begged to be touched. He seemed more innocent than anything, wide-eyed, peaches and cream sweet, and Leah wanted nothing more than to taste that innocence on his lips and skin, even though she knew his history and that there was nothing innocent about the man. The images running through her mind made her palms itch, wanting to shove him against the nearest available surface. He was intoxicating, in the most literal sense of the word.

She sighed, clearing her head. She was here to solve a mystery, not perv on Robert Burns.

"A Guardian is dead," she said, clearing her throat. "The Nuckelavee, leaving that part of Glasgow open to attack. An Attendant was killed – a brownie. Sebastian said that it wasn't his work, and the real mystery was to do with why Dylan was called. So here we are. Dylan was called because the Nuckelavee left its post and came here to die, but the brownie Attendant died first. That means it was probably the Nuckelavee's Attendant."

She walked back and forth across the room. The first tendrils of a purple dawn were beginning to make themselves known through the frost on the window.

"Monster passports," she continued. "Immigration. Anti-immigration? Do monsters have prejudices against other monsters? What are they suspected of? Drug running? Does that mean the brownie that Tearlach found was taking fae opium? But why would that bother the Nuckelavee, unless it was also addicted? We saw a *lot* of Attendants up here, Dorian said they'd be here for the trial but that seemed like too many. Maybe they really are interested in the fate of one selkie, but that looked a lot more like a queue for something. But if only the Attendants were addicted, the person would have had to kill them to get to the Guardians, so they must be linked somehow –"

Leah stood still as Chief Ben's words came back to her in a rush.

"Even the faeries have drug problems..."

She ran out of her hotel room and pounded on Dorian's door. He answered, looking more annoyed than before. She pushed the door open to see a room with a roaring fire in the fireplace, a large armchair in front of it. She turned to him in disbelief, taking in his silk smoking jacket and slippers.

"Okay, Masterpiece Theatre," she said, walking into his room and throwing herself into the chair.

"Excuse me, Leah, but that's my ch –" he began.

"Find another one," she interrupted.

Dorian sighed, and sat down across from her. She noted the glass of whisky by the fire.

"To what do I owe the dubious pleasure of this interruption?" he asked.

"What aren't you telling me, Dorian?" she asked. "You've been secretive since we got here."

"What do you mean?" he asked, but there was a slight quaver to his voice.

"The Guardians," she said. "You said the Attendants are bound to them. Physically?"

"I'm not quite sure what you mean," said Dorian. "They aren't shackled, in any case. They do share a physical connection – or maybe a spiritual one."

"That's what I thought," she said. "You need to tell me more about fae opium. If the Nuckelavee was bound to its Attendants, then the brownie may have died because of their connection."

"I don't know if that's possible," said Dorian. "Addiction is a personal thing. The Fae are usually unaffected by drugs, but –"

"But fae opium was different," Leah finished for him. "Or there wouldn't have been a war."

Dorian stood from his chair and went to the window. He was quiet for so long Leah wondered if he had decided their talk was over.

"Yes," he said, in a soft voice, as if she weren't there. "I thought our drug epidemic was all over. The war ended years ago. We do get a few addicts, of course, mostly in the large cities, but nothing like in the old days of the runners."

"Runners?" asked Leah. "What, like during Prohibition?"

"Yes," said Dorian, "but instead of Prohibition, there was a war. The largest scale war that Faerie has ever seen, and those that were not dying by the needle were dying by the sword. It lasted for centuries. We never thought we'd see the end of it."

Dorian turned back to face her.

"The runners dealt in Fae opium. Our Great War was over the use of a drug, and the runners served addicts on both sides. At first, no one knew how dangerous it was," he explained. "It was common. Fae used to keep it in their kitchens, the same way humans once did with cocaine, in jars on the counter alongside the sugar."

"What is it, Dorian?" asked Leah. "The drug? You call it *opium* but I don't think it's quite the same."

"It is opium, in a sense," Dorian said, "but not the human kind. It is ingested the same way, through injection or inhalation. Most of the Fae who partook in the drug preferred the inhalation method, especially those who wanted to flaunt their use of it. Eventually everyone simply came to call it *the Smoke*."

"So, if the Guardian and the Attendant were linked," Leah asked, "then if one had overdosed, could the other die?"

"Technically, yes," said Dorian. "But we haven't seen fae opium in centuries, and I did not want to believe it had returned, because the true danger is not to the Fae."

"Let me guess who it was dangerous to," said Leah flatly. She already knew the answer, but she wanted to hear Dorian say it.

"Like anything the Fae do, there are ripples that effect entire worlds, universes," said Dorian. "Especially the human one."

"How?" Leah asked.

"You may have heard of the Black Death," Dorian said.

Leah stared at him.

"That was…because of you?" she asked. "Because the Fae liked to get high?"

"Because the Fae got addicted," Dorian said. "The effects of the drug mimic the bubonic plague, but aren't the same. Those humans feeling the effects were beyond saving, even for us. Ingestion of the smoke would cause humans to weaken and die, and since many of us smoked it around humans – in clubs, bars, indeed even opium dens – they couldn't have known to get away from it. We didn't know ourselves, for a while, because of the Plague itself which caused similar reactions. Everyone assumed it was the same thing until it became obvious they were two different problems with similar symptoms."

Dorian sighed.

"As on Earth, so in Heaven," he said, "and the other way around as well. We are often beings of pleasure, in any way that is available to us. It did no good to indulge in the Smoke, but we didn't know it was addictive until we were addicts."

"Did you?" ask Leah. "Did you ever use it?"

Dorian smiled slightly.

"No," he said. "All of my addictions were more...human in nature."

"You'll have to tell me about that sometime," said Leah.

"Later," said Dorian, picking up the thread of his story again, "We did not realise the devastating effect it had on the rest of the world until it was too late. The plague doctors, who believed the Black Death was spread via *miasma*, were half right. Those who died from the Smoke did indeed contract it from bad air."

Leah thought of the reason she'd had to leave Glasgow – the woman dying in the Bridgeton close.

"Dorian," Leah said, "that woman – the woman who died in Dylan's arms. Her fingers were black."

"Yes," he said, "That is why we brought you here – just in case."

It was Leah's turn to stand.

"You need to tell me things," she said. "This is unfair on me, and I had no knowledge of any of this history. I study folklore, and I'm a police officer. Sure, I don't know the history of the Fae the way you do but I don't understand why you didn't feel it necessary to share this information with your partner."

"I thought it would be better this way," he said.

"You don't make decisions for me, Dorian Grey," she said. "I don't care if you're still stuck in your Victorian sensibilities. If we are meant to work as a team, keeping things from me is unhealthy and dangerous, for both of us."

The fire crackled, and Dorian did not respond. He sat like a carved statue, expressionless.

"Goodnight, Dorian."

"Good night."

***

The following morning, they entered the pub. Robert turned and looked at them, throwing a towel over his shoulder. A lazy grin spread across his features as he leaned against the bar.

"Hello, Miss Bishop," he said, making it sound like a come-on.

Leah grinned back at him wolfishly.

"I can't take you anywhere," said Dorian.

"Shut up," Leah whispered. "Do you see those biceps?"

"Leah, it's *Robert Burns*," Dorian pointed out.

The realisation of what this implied was like ice water on Leah's libido. This man was the equivalent of the town bicycle. And this was before the age of modern medicine.

"Oh," she said, faintly disappointed. "Right."

"Would you like breakfast before we go?" Robert asked, apparently having missed the exchange, or polite enough not to comment. "Maybe a drink? Whisky?"

Leah was about to agree when Dorian intervened.

"No," he said. "We are ready."

Leah turned to him, surprised.

"Are we?" she asked.

"As you wish," said Robert.

"Did Robert Burns just quote *The Princess Bride*?" asked Leah.

"I have no idea what you are talking about," said Dorian.

"You've been alive all this time and you want me to believe that you know nothing about pop culture?" asked Leah.

"Should I?" asked Dorian. Leah considered this.

"You know, on second thought," she said, "a lot of it is useless."

"How surprising," said Dorian.

Robert opened the door to the bar.

"This just seems to be the type of relationship we have," said Leah. "I follow you into weird new worlds. Like into the broom closet. Real magical introduction to Interpol, by the way."

"But you're never bored," said Robert over her shoulder, winking. Despite her attraction, Leah fixed him with a hard look.

"I wouldn't try it," said Leah. "I've read your story."

"*Touché*," said Robert, totally on board with everyone knowing he'd once gotten into the pants of half the people in Scotland.

Robert turned and pushed the door behind the bar open, flooding the room with bright light.

"After you," he said.

"The door to Faerie is…behind a bar?" asked Leah.

"It makes perfect sense, when you think about it," said Dorian.

"Maybe in Scotland," Leah huffed.

Dorian walked forward first, and Leah followed. Robert went last, closing the door behind him.

The world spins.

They are in a field, unbelievably bright and filled with flowers. The sun is warm, a drowsy afternoon. Leah is breathless.

"So, here we are," Robert said. "Home again, after all this time, Dorian."

Dorian sniffed.

"This is not my home. It is further to the West."

Robert leaned over to Leah conspiratorially.

"Selkies are the aristocrats of our world," he said. "Once Taken, they can be unbelievably insufferable. The islands to the West have been the land of Faerie for a long time, but the selkies claim seniority because their islands are further West."

"Hmph," said Dorian.

"Go west far enough, and you hit America," said Leah. "And, well, the rest of the world, eventually."

"Indeed," he said, noncommittal. "One day, perhaps, you will see the Home-place. Seal-hame is beautiful."

"Also, you'd drown," said Robert. "It's underwater."

There were three pathways in front of them, stretching off and away through the green into the distance. One was dirt, one was of broken cobblestones, and one was paved. Out of the corner of her eye, Leah could see Robert smiling at her. *Man, you could fall in love with those eyes*, she thought.

"Which road?" she said out loud.

Robert folded his arms.

"This is Faerie," he said. "You're a folklorist. You must remember."

"Studying something and being in it are two different things," she said. "It's like spending years studying China, but you have no idea how to ask for rice at the grocery store."

"There are three paths," said Dorian. "Which would you choose?"

Leah looked around at the beautiful field. In the distance, a loch sparkled in the sunlight, and the sky was a deep blue.

"Well, in my studies, the wide road, the middle road, was the road to Faerie. There was some idea that since faeries may not have predated Christianity, this was an allusion to Purgatory – much like the faeries were considered half-fallen angels, too good for Hell, too evil for Heaven."

She went to the place where the roads forked.

"But in all the stories, there was only the middle road...if I was to guess, it is the narrow path that leads to Heaven, or to Elysium. That is a different kind of folklore, but I also believe there is a great deal of convergence."

"That's fairly accurate," said Dorian, "but what about the third road?"

"Hell, I assume?" she said. "I don't really think it looks tempting enough, or evil enough, to be Hell."

Robert's grin broadened.

"The answer is...none of these roads lead anywhere," he said. "They just turn back on themselves, or vanish, like a mirage. We're already there. The place likes to become what you expect it to be. It's human imagination that drives it – that drives us all."

Leah considered this, and began to smile, a mischievous grin. Dorian recognised the look and opened his mouth to speak.

"So if I wish very, *very* hard..." she said.

Dorian was suddenly wearing a T-shirt and jeans. He wrapped his arms around his body as if he were naked. Robert was shirtless, gooseflesh spreading across his skin, his muscular chest expanding with his breath. He looked extremely pleased with himself, which dimmed Leah's enjoyment of the experience a bit.

"Excuse me! Leah!" Dorian said. Robert grinned.

"I like it already," said Leah.

As the wish faded, the two men returned to their normal state of being, and Dorian glared daggers at her for a while. Robert took a key out of his pocket and inserted it into what looked like thin air in front of them. He turned the key, and with a groaning sound, a door opened in the midst of the field and they stepped through it, entering what looked like the court of a king.

The entire room was filled with selkies. Handsome men of all descriptions, shapes, and sizes, with one defining feature – they were all dark-haired, and dark-eyed. Paintings of seals surrounded the hall, and the windows let in bright sunlight that moved backwards across the day, and sometimes looked the way it did underwater, flowing and changing, shattered. Leah realised, suddenly, that the hall was under the ocean.

"Why are there only selkies here?" asked Leah. "There are so many different types of Fae."

"Tried by a jury of your peers," Dorian explained. "One of the better human inventions, I think."

The man seated on the throne was incredible. His long hair fell like a silk sheet over his shoulder, and he wore silver raiment, a coat so fine it looked as though it had been spun from stars. His cheekbones were high and regal, and his dark eyes soft yet stern.

"That is the Seal-King," said Dorian, bowing low with the others.

The Seal-King leaned forward on his throne.

"Bring Magnus Grey before the court."

Everyone present turned. Leah gasped.

It had been a year since she had seen Magnus Grey. Gorgeous and confident, with foxy eyes and Botticelli curls, there were few men or selkies that could claim to outdo him.

Not so now.

He was thin, and looked ill; his clothes hung off him, his hair in disarray, he looked like the ghost of the man he had been. He was, however, still beautiful, an angelic face that gave lie to the things he was capable of.

"You stand accused of the serial murder of humans belonging to the Taken selk," said the Seal-King. "How do you plead, Magnus Grey?"

"Guilty as charged, Your Majesty," said Magnus in a weak voice.

"Have you nothing to say in your defence?" asked the King.

Magnus's large eyes surveyed the room, and stopped, as he choked a little upon seeing Dorian and Leah in the gallery. Dorian looked away, and Magnus hung his head.

"No," he said, "I have disappointed my people, and most of all, my brother Dorian."

"Dorian Grey," the Seal-King's smooth baritone rolled across the audience, "is there anything you would like to say on your brother's behalf?"

Dorian stared down at the King and said nothing.

"Very well," said the King, "The court is adjourned. The punishment will be announced in the morning."

CHAPTER SIX

ater, upon their return from Faerie, Leah slid into a seat at the hotel bar. Dorian sat across from her.

"Robert, could I get a whisky?" she asked, "Bruichladdich, please."

"Sure," he replied, busying himself behind the bar.

"Something wrong?" asked Dorian.

"You just sat there, while they were trying Magnus," said Leah. "You sat there and you didn't say a word! He's your *brother*, Dorian!"

"Magnus is a killer," said Dorian, "and any attraction you felt towards him was only a part of the selkie charm."

"I know that," she replied. "It's not Magnus I am worried about, it's you. It's like you are completely devoid of emotion, except for loving this woman from years ago. Don't you care?"

"Yes. I certainly care," said Dorian. "However, Magnus made his choice. I cannot let my feelings get in the way of my job as a police officer."

Robert walked over to the table and set down glasses of whisky.

"They'll kill him, you know," he said. "You're all right with that?"

"I'm not *all right* with it, no," said Dorian. "But if that is what the tribunal decides, then that is the punishment Magnus will have to accept."

"Wow," said Leah. "I sure hope I never get on your bad side. You are as cold as a fish. You don't care about anything."

"Hmmm, fish," said Dorian. "Robert, do you still have that salmon?"

"Fresh from the burn this morning," Robert replied.

Leah shook her head, sipping her drink, as Robert disappeared into the kitchen. Dorian sipped at his own whisky without comment.

Robert returned with the food, and a glass of whisky for himself. He sat down across from Leah.

"So, Dorian tells me you've got your heart set on someone," said Leah. "Old memories or new love?"

"Old," said Robert. "I was always such a romantic. But the woman who made me like this? I will never forget her. I had many lovers, as you seem to know, and I loved them all. But..."

"She was the one?" asked Leah, charmed.

"Well, she was the one who introduced me to this other world," said Robert. "No one could really impress me afterwards."

"What happened to her?" Leah asked.

Robert's eyes had a faraway look.

"She was exiled."

***

The young man opened the door to the pub.

It was dark inside, as always. The crackling scent of the peat fire tickled his nose as he entered the pub's suffocating warmth. The walls were blackened from years of smoke, from the peat-fire, from the pipes. The wooden tables and chairs made up a sparse environment, but the attraction here were the inhabitants rather than the decoration. It was Tarbolton, after all, not much more than a tiny farming village unheard of by the rest of the world.

One day, the young man from Alloway with the dirty face and torn clothing would be the reason the world had heard of Ayrshire.

He sat down at a table, unsure of himself. He had a few coins in his pocket but that was all. His stern father believed him to be too much of a dreamer, always mooning after young women and not keeping his mind on his work. He sighed, and scrubbed a hand over his face. It had been a long, hard day. They all were, for a ploughman; up before dawn, backbreaking work in the fields until it was too dark to see. His family was poor, and he was often hungry. His clothes hung off his frame. He would be handsome – devilishly so – if he'd been well-fed and taken care of. As it was, he simply looked gaunt, peering out at the world with too-large doe eyes that broadcast his innocence to the universe, and made him the perfect victim.

"Can I buy you a drink?" rumbled a deep voice near his elbow.

He looked into eyes so green he couldn't believe they were real. Even in the darkness of the pub, they shone like translucent jade. The hard lines of the man's face spoke of a harsh life, and the pipe he held in one hand curled smoke as he put it to soft, full lips.

"Yes?" said the young man cautiously. He wondered why he'd focused on the man's mouth.

"What're you having?" asked the man.

"Wh – whisky," Robert stammered.

"Like your eyes," said the man, dropping him a wink, and pushed off towards the bar.

Robert's mouth hung open. Did the man just –

"Robert," said another voice. This voice he knew – it was an old friend.

"Richard," Robert nodded.

"It's all been arranged," Captain Richard Brown said. He was well-known among the ladies, cutting a dashing, dark figure, and Robert always felt at a loss around him. Richard had decided to take the young man in hand and show him the joys of what he called *illicit love*.

"Richard," said Robert, starting to panic, "I really don't think that's –"

"Robert," said Richard, insistent, "You are made for more than this. You have a real talent! You'll be a great poet one day, you'll see. But the only way anyone is ever going to know about your poetry is if you stand up and read it."

"My father –" Robert protested. Richard sighed.

"Your father is not your king and commander!" he said. "He can't live forever. No one can."

Two glasses of whisky were set down on the table by hands that were pale and ivory-white. Robert looked up into those green eyes, sparkling merrily at him. His breath caught in his throat, and he didn't know why.

"So you're a poet," said the stranger, taking a seat across from him.

Richard nodded, winking, and made himself scarce. Robert stared after him with questioning eyes. He turned back to the stranger, who was watching him, a smile playing about his features.

"I – sometimes I write," Robert said. Those eyes were *so green*, he thought. Like the fields in the springtime, just after the first rains –

"He mentioned you're doing a recitation?" asked the man.

"Yes," Robert mumbled. He sipped his whisky, wondering if that was why he felt off-balance and a little dizzy. "Next week. Richard is...forceful."

The man grinned. Robert's heart nearly stopped.

"Man after my own heart," the stranger said. "So. What do you know about monsters?"

Robert cleared his throat and stuttered. His mind was swimming, images that scandalised him rushing through it like water, so vivid and filthy they didn't even seem to come from him. He was having trouble focusing on anything apart from this man's lips around the stem of the pipe, and the devastating green of his eyes.

"M – monsters?" he asked.

"You'll have to work on that," said the other man, taking a pull of his pipe. Robert's eyes started to water. "You're never going to be able to recite poetry if you're nervous. You remind me of a snake charmer I met in Penang once. Told me he couldn't handle the snakes if he was scared and they always knew. Almost got killed by his king cobra, too. They can sense it, Faisal said."

Robert's eyes were wide, his consciousness latching onto something among the torrent of erotic thoughts currently cascading through his mind.

"You've been to Malay?" he asked. The entire world opened up like a gulf at his feet when the man nodded and grinned.

"Yes," he replied.

"People aren't snakes," Robert said then. The man just quirked an eyebrow.

"Where...where else have you been?" Robert asked.

"You're very handsome," said the man suddenly, ignoring his question. "It's breathtaking, really."

Robert stared. He'd never heard anyone say something so direct to anyone else, man or woman. There was a coiled strength in this man, whoever he was; quiet and calm but clear as the build of an ocean wave that could rain down desolation, an unexpected force of nature, irresistible, resisting. His eyes were so green Robert was having trouble believing they were real, lit up from within, as though the man was made of light, barely contained and beautiful.

However, at this point in Robert's career as a poet, what came out was "Er?"

"Some island cultures don't have bards to speak of," the man continued, as if he hadn't just destroyed Robert's composure, "but they sing their histories, and they believe that if you can't do that yourself, you have no soul."

"Where else have you been?" Robert repeated.

The man grinned.

"Everywhere," he replied. Robert was lost.

The man began to recite stories from across Scotland, from across time, and Robert was drowning. Adventure did not often come to Ayrshire, and until tonight, Robert had consigned himself to the dreary existence of a ploughman in a tiny corner of the world, his heart full of love and poetry but also the knowledge that poetry and love weren't going to get the chores done. Robert wondered, briefly, through the haze of alcohol, if

65

there was something fey about the man, because he was hypnotised, swaying, falling…drowning, drowning in that eternal green.

"But what about you?" asked the man.

Robert was jolted back to reality.

"M – me?" he asked. "What do you mean?"

"Tell me about yourself," said the man. "What do you do? You write poetry, but about what? Have you ever been anywhere outside of Scotland?"

"Why?" asked Robert, defensive. Nobody had ever asked him about himself before. Nobody had cared. He was just a stupid peasant farmer, one of countless thousands living out the eternal birth-to-death cycle of working the fields so the rich could eat, pausing on the way to create children and perpetuate the monotony.

"Because," said the man, grinning, leaning closer, conspiratorial, "that's how you make friends."

Robert could feel the man's whisper, a tactile thing now that he was nearer, and his skin pebbled as the man's soft breath ghosted across his skin.

"Well," Robert began, "I was born here in Ayr – in Alloway – my mum said that the door blew open when I was born, the wind was so strong. I live with my parents on our farm and – but this is very boring, you don't want to hear this."

The man only leaned forward further, engrossed, as if Robert's story was just as interesting as his endless travels, as if Robert was a thing both beautiful and beloved. Those lips, those eyes, so much closer now, close enough to touch if he just leaned in –

Robert took a deep breath and continued.

"My father and I don't get on," he began. "He doesn't approve of the poetry – he doesn't think it's worth much to a poor farmer. I can't help it, it's just there. I'm just compelled to write. I don't think I could stop even if I tried."

Robert must not have realised how much he needed this, because he poured out his life and soul to this man who sat there looking at him, smiling fondly, not interrupting. He laughed when the story was funny, his brow creased when the story was sad. As Robert talked, he took in the careworn lines on his companion's face, on the hands, the fingers wrapped delicately around the stem of the pipe, and sensed that this man had suffered greatly, and for a long time; he could read this unspoken sorrow in the drawn-down cast of his mouth, especially when Robert talked about his own difficulties. The man's expression would change, subtle and fierce. *Military*, Robert thought at one point, *or a warrior built of other blood and bone.*

The man kept buying him drinks – good whisky, too, not the terrible low-quality kind Robert could afford, but the type that was usually kept away from most of Ayr society and brought out only for weddings or visiting dignitaries. As the night wore on, he grew bolder; his shyness falling away, and he began to talk with feeling.

The man simply sat there and listened, drawing on the pipe and gently exhaling smoke, from a mouth Robert first thought was beautiful and then was hungry for. As he watched those lips tighten around the stem of the pipe once again, Robert forgot where he was, who he was, he forgot about his father or his poetry or his future or past. He wanted to touch those lips with his, to breathe the smoke into himself, to take this man into himself.

Somewhere a voice in his head was speaking in a frantic tattoo:

what are you doing, this is Tarbolton, this is your local, the vicar is probably still here – what you are doing is illegal – men get hung for this – Robert get ahold of yourself

and he leaned forward, wanting to taste that mouth as the other man dropped the pipe from his lips and breathed out, tendrils of smoke rising around a face lined with sorrow and darkness.

The other man abruptly stood, offering his hand to Robert.

"You'd better get home," he said, and Robert was startled out of his reverie. He noticed the loud ringing of the bell that signified closing time. He groaned. His father would be very angry, as he had never stayed out quite so late before – nor had he ever been quite so drunk before. It was not alcohol that ran fire and light through his veins, and he allowed the man to lead him out the door. In the darkness, the man bowed to him, and Robert watched him walk away, smoke curling around him like a lover, until he disappeared into the darkness.

Robert turned in a daze, taking the path through the forest that lead to his farm. As he fell into his bed that night, alight with love, he suddenly realised he'd never asked for the man's name.

He woke to sunlight streaming into his room, and groaned with a headache that pounded through his entire body.

"Robert!" his father was calling. He sat up quickly, and immediately regretted it. He was late – very late – and the field needed ploughing. He was going to hate today.

As he pushed the plough forward with all his strength, thanking God and his angels for the sticky porridge breakfast he'd never much liked before, he considered the events of the previous night.

You just fell in love, said his mind, *with a man*.

Robert considered this, worried.

Did that mean anything? He had heard of it before. He considered.

He could not deny the way his heart felt, his entire being, and he decided that his current goal in life was to get the man's name. He wondered if he would be interested, or horrified, or if he felt the same.

He compared my eyes to whisky, thought Robert fondly. *And I know I will see him again, because I am going to recite my poetry, and he promised he would not miss it for the world.*

Determined, Robert Burns ploughed the fields, and for the first time looked forward to his performance.

***

Robert stood in front of the pub, wishing he'd been able to have a whisky to calm his nerves.

The chill of the cold grey evening had dampened his skin, his arms clammy; he did not even have a plaid to keep himself warm. He had soldiered on to the pub and the warmth he knew was waiting. If the audience liked his poem, he hoped they'd buy him enough whisky to convince him he was warm inside on his long walk back to the farm later that night.

It seemed like everyone in town was there in the audience, wearing sceptical expressions. He huffed a breath and stared down at his hands to give himself something to do. *What are you waiting for?* he accused himself. *Start talking!* He pulled at the ends of his loose shirtsleeves, thinking he should probably have washed his face. The crowd was beginning to murmur and his nerves were getting the best of him.

His heart leapt in his chest when he saw through the smoke, as someone pushed through the door into the warm, cloying darkness of the pub.

There was the man he had met, sitting where he'd promised to be, at one of the dark wooden tables nearest the leaping fire. Robert felt his heart twist when he saw another man sitting next to him, a man of slender stature and such intense beauty he wondered if the other patrons had noticed. Jealousy streaked through his veins before he was quite aware of what he was feeling; was this other man a lover? A friend? Either way he'd known those green, green eyes longer than Robert had, and it made him irrationally jealous.

And then the man looked at him – those bright, too-bright green eyes glowed like embers, and Robert recovered his strength, his confidence, as Richard came up to him, grinned and shook his hand, and almost pushed Robert in front of the audience.

But Robert only had eyes for one person in the crowd.

Robert knew he was in love, believed with all his soul that he was in love with a man, and in that moment, he did not care.

Robert Burns opened his mouth, and began to recite his poetry for the first time, in a history that would follow him down.

The small pub was loud, and rowdy. Desdemona sat in a corner watching the proceedings, as a young poet stood up to read his work. She was dressed a man, and to all outside appearances looked like a man.

Her companion was the most beautiful creature on the physical plane, then or now. Nothing had ever been birthed with the kind of beauty this young man possessed, flawless skin and wide dark eyes. People found it difficult to look at him, because he shone.

Desdemona was a *baobhan sith* vampire, and although technically genderless, her people appeared to be human women. *The White Women of the Highlands.*

Her companion, Iain, was the most beautiful selkie ever born.

He was also unimpressed.

"Desdemona," he said, "We don't have time for this."

"Come on, Iain," she said, "we don't get a lot of time away from the garrison. Anyway, he's handsome, and I've heard he's talented."

"Don't you have enough young men?" asked Iain.

Desdemona grinned at him, the white stem of her pipe between her teeth.

"Is there such a thing?" she asked. He smirked.

"Why don't you just kill him? Why do you need to drag it out?" he asked.

"Because then I don't get to see the look on his face when I eat him," Desdemona said around her pipe as she lit it. She drew smoke into her lungs and breathed out, like a dragon.

The young poet stood on the stage, nervous. He had already noticed Desdemona, who grinned boldly at him through the wreath of smoke with her bright and strange green eyes. Her gaze nailed him to the wall. He stuttered, and began to recite.

As I was a-wand'ring ae morning in spring,
Ae heard a young ploughman sae sweetly tae sing...

Iain side-eyed Desdemona with a stare of disbelief. Desdemona, for her part, dropped a wink at the man in the front of the pub. Unfortunately, she seemed to be the only one present interested in the proceedings.

The other patrons seemed to share Iain's sentiment, as they were getting rowdier by the moment.

"Oh, give it a rest, Robert! ... who cares?... *You just wait til your da hears about this!* Go home, Robert!"

Robert, for his part, had seen Desdemona wink and felt strengthened for a moment. He ventured to continue.

And as he was singin', thir words he did say,

there's nae life like a ploughman's in the month of sweet May...

But the angry, derisive shouts of the other denizens of the pub drowned out his words.

These were people he'd have to see, he realised, tomorrow and every day after, when he had to go to town to fetch the shopping for his mother or to ask the landlord yet again to give his father more time on the rent. Tarbolton and rural Scotland were all the future held for him, and these were the people he'd have to face in the light of day.

Robert, onstage, faltered to a stop. He dropped his head in shame, the unkempt strands of hair hiding his scarlet cheeks. He pushed his way through the jeering crowd and out the door, hiding in his humiliation in the cold darkness of a winter's night.

Robert walked alone, listening to the crunch of his footfalls on the path. He wiped at tears that stung his eyes, unbidden, making tracks through the dirt on his face. He sighed as he noticed it rub off onto his white shirt cuffs. Robert couldn't see his way in the darkness, but that was fine; he knew his way back and forth from the farm to the pub and would be able to navigate it in his sleep.

He sighed deeply, feeling like an idiot. He lived in the middle of nowhere. He was a ploughman's son, in a tiny village no one had ever heard of. It was ridiculous of Richard Brown to talk him into this. He ought to have listened to his father, and dedicated himself to the plough instead. He was physically strong, enough for the town to talk of it, and he was talented in his work. Unfortunately, Robert's heart desired more than the hard farmer's life he had watched ruin his father. He had other interests, and had spent his entire life at the plough. He didn't want to offer up the rest of it as a kind of sacrifice to the land. As it was, he already had a bit of a stoop when he walked, so he had felt like he'd given enough to the earth.

Robert was so wrapped in his own thoughts that he hadn't noticed the quiet snick of breaking branches underfoot, or sensed that something was following him.

The Nuckelavee was on him with a terrible roar before he was even aware what was happening. He threw his arms over his face protectively but could do nothing more as the great beast snapped at him with its long, scything teeth. As the Nuckelavee leaned down toward him, Robert could feel its hot breath on his face. He felt no inclination to fight or flee; he felt his life only a small candle flame to be snuffed out. It was not as if he would be worth much in the grand scheme of things, nor the history of the world.

The *crack* of gunfire and the monster's yelp as it leapt and rolled away into the trees at the side of the path stunned him. He had been certain he was a dead man. He looked up cautiously, to see the man who had been in his thoughts for days, and his beautiful young male companion.

His eyes moved from one of them to the other, wondering about their relationship. His heartbeat began to slow to a more natural rhythm.

"Good evening, Robert Burns," said the man with green eyes. "I'm Desdemona. That's Iain. Faeries exist, and we are at war."

Desdemona. Robert gaped at… *her?* She put out a hand to help him up.

"And by the way...happy birthday."

Robert was dazed, but the first stirrings of amazement in his heart were leading down a path he did not want to think about. *Not a man…but some kind of Fae warrior.*

That's not any better, Robert, he chided himself.

"I liked your poem," said the one called Desdemona.

He found it hard to believe she was a woman while he looked at her, so much did she resemble a man. A handsome man, certainly, but a man all the same.

"Thank you. I think you may be the only one," said Robert.

"He's right, I hated it," said Iain mildly.

"Thank you, Iain," Desdemona said in a world-weary voice.

***

Robert Burns never had any difficulty falling in love.

Truth be told, it didn't take much.

And there stood Desdemona, gun still smoking, beside her beautiful lieutenant. She favoured Robert with a cocky grin as her eyes raked over him. He had never been looked at in that way by anyone, man or woman.

And it turned out that she was indeed a woman. But he had already decided that it didn't matter.

"Can I come with you?" was the first question out of Robert's mouth.

Desdemona raised an eyebrow.

"You're human," she said. "Go back to your plough, little poet. Live a long and happy life. Have many children. Get rich and famous off your work. Travel. See the world."

She and Iain holstered their pistols.

"And forget you ever saw us, Robert Burns," she said. She turned to Iain.

"Ready to go, General?" he asked, and she nodded curtly.

The two Fae soldiers murmured to each other as they walked away from Robert. He knew they thought he couldn't hear them, but he could.

Why didn't you kill him? I thought you were going to eat him.

I was. He looks like he'd taste good. Prime steak.

Then why didn't you? Desdemona…

I don't know, Iain.

The vampire looked off into the distance, as if she had surprised even herself.

I don't know.

***

As they walked away from him down the path, Robert saw Desdemona look over her shoulder and wink at him. Even from a distance, he could still see that preternatural green lighting the darkness.

Robert was rooted to the spot for the moment. He knew the dangers of the Fae, of following them into the darkness, of losing years of life to the passion they inspired in men. His mother was a wise, sensible woman who had made sure he was instructed in all of the fairy and folktales of the country people. He knew how foolish it would be to follow her in secret and that only an idiot would blatantly ignore the advice of a clearly powerful Fae creature.

He followed her down the path, his heart beating with the first wash of love.

***

Robert peered around the bushes, eager to see what a Fae war looked like. His excited imagination provided him with a fantastical light show, incredible displays of power, and feats of bravery, with Desdemona in the centre of it all – whatever kind of creature she might be – powerful, with a terrible beauty.

He did not expect what greeted his eyes.

Row upon row of makeshift cots, creatures of all shapes and descriptions laying on them, groaning or sighing. Several of these – monsters? – were missing limbs, or were screaming as another monster stitched a wound back together. In one case, a creature appeared to be having an eye sewn back into his head by a grey-blue man with the most hideous face Robert had ever seen.

74

In the midst of it all, Desdemona knelt by the side of what Robert's limited knowledge identified as an elf. Beautiful, his eyes stared out, glassy, as she held him down. Her fingernails grew into long talons and she pierced his neck, leaning down to drink.

"She's *baobhan sith*," he whispered to himself. "*She's a vampire.*"

He watched in wonder, however, as she did not drink the elf's blood, but collected it in a pan. She leaned over and put her hand to the elf's forehead, staring down through those bright green eyes, and even from this distance Robert could see the anguish on her face. Shaking her head slightly, she took the blood collected in the pan and brought it to another elf, shaking and screaming in pain, and introduced it to the gaping wound in his stomach. Light bled out from the wound, but the body accepted it, and the wound began to heal itself as several monsters held the elf down in order to allow the painful healing process to begin.

The elf's stomach began to pull itself together after the offering of blood, and Desdemona stood watch as the young man wept and shrieked in agony. Her eyes never left his, and Robert remembered drowning in that endless green, the first night in the pub where he had seen her and fallen. The elf slowly quieted, hypnotised by the green in her eyes, and while his body continued to work the wound closed, the screams abated into sighs, and then languid breathing.

The elf looked down. He was whole again.

He sighed, collapsing against the other monsters holding him down.

"Desdemona," said the elf, weary, "*Thank you.*"

She nodded to him, and turned away, toward where Robert was hiding.

"We're killing each other," she muttered, "over this."

He was startled to see her angrily brush at her eyes, tears dimming the preternatural green radiating there, moonlight through a stained-glass window.

She was almost close enough to touch…

A hideous grey-blue face appeared in front of his and Robert cried out in surprise and terror.

"Desdemona," said the monster, "look what I found."

***

"I told you not to follow us," said Desdemona.

"That was very unwise," said the ugly grey-blue creature, whose name was Gregoire. "Your penchant for these handsome young men, Desdemona –"

"Yes, yes," Desdemona said, waving this away. "I got hungry. I wasn't being careful."

Iain stared at Robert, as he polished his gun.

"You want me to kill him, General?" asked Iain.

"There's no need for theatrics," said Desdemona.

Robert knelt on the ground in front of her, his head bowed.

Desdemona looked down at this man, kneeling in the mud, his face smudged with dirt.

"Look at me, Robert," she said, and he looked up into her eyes with a love so sharp and honest she nearly took a step back.

"Oh," she said softly, in a voice that almost sounded like it was not her own.

Iain glared at him, cocking his weapon.

"There's been enough bloodshed," she said. "Put the gun away, Iain."

Desdemona knelt down in front of Robert, who was about to protest. He would kneel there before her forever, he knew this in his heart; this imperious queen could not be brought so low as to look into his eyes as if they were equals.

"Do with me what you will," he breathed, his heart pounding, less from fear than from her proximity.

"Gregoire, Iain," she said. "Leave us."

"General…" Iain started.

"Iain, go," said Desdemona.

Iain reluctantly stood.

"I'll be right next to the first row of cots if you need me," Iain said.

"I won't tell you again," said Desdemona. Her green eyes never left Robert's face, searching.

"Come on," said Gregoire, turning the young lieutenant's shoulder toward the camp, "she'll be safe."

"But –" Iain began. Robert didn't hear what his protest was, as he was led away into the general cacophony of the clearing that served as the medical bay for the Fae battalion.

Robert dropped his gaze, staring at the ground. He felt that he would be consumed from within, by that green and strange fire, by the way his world had contracted, expanded, and fallen in upon himself, and by the treachery of his poet's heart.

"Look at me, Robert," Desdemona commanded, and all he could do was obey.

He lifted his eyes and was caught, snake-charmed and pinned, and he knew he would do anything she asked. If it were impossible, he would kill himself trying.

The pain behind her eyes was more than he could bear. His own eyes filled with tears, ready to throw himself on whatever had given her that endless stare.

"Go home, Robert Burns," she said, her voice cracking.

They knelt there together, the young, handsome, lovestruck idiot, newly adult, newly human, and the war-torn battle veteran, impossibly ancient, indescribably old, pale and powerful. They reflected each other, and for once in the godforsaken history of that war, it was the awkward, brash, and human love that won. Desdemona had seen thousands of years like this one and would see thousands more. Robert had only a handful of years. This was the first time the love of Robert Burns transcended darkness, immortality, and destiny, as he stared back at her and into that endless abyss of green.

"No," he whispered, and the sound of his defiance was loud in the clearing, even with the sick bay and the sounds of war. The world was hushed to hear the voice of this foolish youth who had walked bodily into the fire so it could consume him and somehow, he stood within it, unscathed.

Desdemona's natural frown deepened. She could think of nothing to say. She knew this young man was different, and she knew then and there that he would cut a path through history so deep the entire world would sing of it one day.

For the time being, though, she lifted him from where he had nearly prostrated himself before her, his hands, the hands of a farmer's son, clinging to the dirt and earth for the last time. His heart still beat with fear; fear of the unknown, despite the desire consuming him. He held to the earth, digging his fingertips deep in the soil. He was reluctant to let go.

She offered him her hand.

"Then join us," she said simply.

He put his hand in hers, and relinquished the earth.

And Robert has never stopped falling.

***

Leah stared at Robert over her glass.

"And that was how I joined the resistance," he said.

"Without even knowing why?" asked Leah. "Or what the war was about?"

"Well, she was captivating. I had a weakness, which is famous by now. And eventually, that's how I met Dorian."

"That must have dragged things down a bit," said Leah. "He's not exactly the life of the party."

"On the contrary," said Dorian. "I was rather different before I was Taken."

Robert grinned.

"Rather," he said. "Dorian *was* the party. And if there wasn't a party, he'd start one. All by himself."

A glass dropped, smashing across the floor. The two men looked at Leah.

"Are you all right?" asked Dorian.

"I think you may have to go to the trial alone, Dorian," she

❀ CHAPTER SIX ❀

managed to say, as she collapsed onto the floor.

CHAPTER SEVEN

Robert rushed into Gregoire's cave, holding Leah in his arms. This would have been disappointing to Leah, both because she was not conscious to experience it and also because her ideas ran more toward the roles being reversed.

"Gregoire! Help us!" shouted Robert.

He set her down on Gregoire's couch. Leah stared up at him, eyes glassy.

"What is it? What's happened? Dorian?" said Gregoire, rushing around a corner to see Leah's still form lying on his sofa. He looked from her to Robert, questioning.

Dorian stood well away, close to the wall, as if he didn't want to get involved.

Robert walked over to Dorian, crowding into his space.

"Dorian, what is going on here?" Robert demanded. "You show up after all these years, and there's no way it's just for your brother's trial. Tell me."

Dorian looked at the floor.

"It's the Smoke, Robert," said Dorian. "It's back."

Both Robert and Gregoire recoiled, the urisk letting out a sound of horror.

"It can't be, Dorian, everyone died a long time ago..." Gregoire said, not wanting to believe his friend.

"I know!" said Dorian in desperation. "But a few days ago, Dylan – the new Guardian – watched a woman die of it in a stairwell. Leah was there. I thought – if we got her out of the city, somewhere near Faerie, she wouldn't ..."

"It's too late now, Dorian!" Robert shouted. "What were you thinking? She must stay here, Gregoire. You were the field medic, back then. You're the only one who knows."

Gregoire nodded.

"Of course."

Robert rounded on Dorian.

"This was irresponsible of you, Dorian! She needs medicine! *Human* medicine!"

Dorian glared at him.

"That never worked either, Robert!" he said. He took out his phone.

"What are you doing now?"

"I'm calling Milo."

***

Down in the heart of Caledonia Interpol, beyond the Minotaur and his labyrinth, Milo worked in silence.

Milo's lab was filled with mysterious things. Strange creatures in cages all along one wall, and bubbling liquids of questionable colours filled every conceivable beaker and phial. Vivisected animals of unknown species and origin lay pinned to various boards. In the distant darkness, the bodies of the morgue could be seen through the gloom.

Milo was a merman, and Caledonia Interpol's resident forensic pathologist. He was a genius, but not averse to soul-eating, as the *ceasg* were wont to do.

Milo sighed. He found working by himself overwhelming, with no one to bounce ideas off or help him with his questionably legal experiments. Finding a reliable assistant wasn't easy; he did most of his work in a secret underground lab and almost never went outside. He missed Geoffrey, but now that they had discovered he was Sebastian, his assistant wasn't coming back. So he worked alone.

He chopped up something phosphorescent and orange, dropping it into a beaker. Something rolled past his hand and he dropped a book in front of it to stop its progress.

His phone rang. He lifted it to his ear.

"Hello, Dorian," he said. He listened for a moment.

"Oh yes," he said. "The false Black Death. It's been so many years since I've seen it. Still, we're able to cure the Black Death these days, and if we're able to isolate the causative agent, it may be possible to deal with the false Black Death as well."

He grabbed another small animal that was making a break for it and firmly locked it into a cage.

"It's not the disease itself that is your biggest concern, of course," said Milo.

"Why's that?" asked Dorian.

"We're as powerless to stop it now as we were back then. I am sorry, but it is only a matter of time," said Milo. "We won't have enough of the cure in stock, whatever it may be, and human doctors are likely treating it as if it's the true bubonic plague. They'll be getting nowhere. Like it or not, this disease may be supernatural in origin, but it is a human sickness. They will quarantine the city. And the monsters will be all that is left."

Dorian blanched.

"You're certain there's nothing we can do?" asked Dorian. "Milo, we're the Fae. The most powerful creatures on earth."

Milo shrugged.

"We are powerless stop it, now as we were then," said Milo. "The Black Death stalks Glasgow. And this is outside our jurisdiction. The humans will not survive."

Dorian shot a horrified look at Robert and Gregoire.

"Still. You say there is a cure," Dorian said. "Could we put it into the water supply?"

"Depending on whether we figured out what strain it is in advance," said Milo. "But you are dealing with humans now, not the Fae. Humans are superstitious and afraid. It is the panic that you will not be able to quell in the coming days."

"How long do we have?" Dorian asked.

"Most cases of the true bubonic plague end in death between two days and one week," he said, "However, the cases we were certain were caused by the Smoke? We never found out. We were a bit distracted by the war at the time."

Dorian sighed and put his hand to his forehead. Dimly, he was aware Milo was speaking to him.

"Dorian," said Milo. "You may have to make this sacrifice."

Dorian clenched his jaw and hung up the phone with a gruff 'thanks'. Robert and Gregoire looked at him in earnest.

"Is there a cure yet?" Gregoire asked.

"There never was," said Robert. "As far as I know, there still isn't."

Dorian nodded.

"Milo says there is nothing he can do," he said. "It's nearly dawn, and I need to go to the trial."

Robert took Dorian aside.

"You care for her, Dorian," he said gently.

Dorian nodded.

"Not in the selkie way, of course," said Dorian. "That was taken long ago – but she is my partner. And she is human."

He suddenly slammed his fist into the table, shaking the little postcards of Scottie dogs and the tartan throws, bagpiper trinkets, and tea tins.

"*She is human,*" Dorian said. "And there's nothing I can do. Faeries, magic, power…all the power in the world, and there's nothing we can do."

***

The sun filtered down, as it always had in the selkie court. Dorian wasn't sure if this was because there were no clouds in Faerie or if the court moved constantly to places where the sun was still shining. The only time he had seen it in darkness was in the evening, when it was lit by thousands of candles.

Anything to light our features well, Dorian thought uncharitably.

His brother was brought out again, the shackles weighing him down. Magnus looked up in hope at the gallery, trying to catch his eye. Dorian ignored him.

"Magnus Grey, we are here to discuss your punishment," said

the handsome Seal-King from his throne.

"You have murdered humans in cold blood, in order to draw attention from yourself, and one you have killed in passion after abusing our powers.

"The court has decreed that you will be sentenced to death by overdose."

Magnus, silent and defeated, bowed his head.

Dorian looked up.

"Your Majesty, if I may?" he said.

Magnus started, lifting his head to look in his brother's direction.

"Let the court recognise Dorian Grey," said the Seal-King.

"Today I discovered that the Smoke has returned," said Dorian.

There was a collective gasp, and a murmur in the court. The Seal-King waved his hand, and there was silence.

"I may have already lost my partner and best friend to the disease," said Dorian. "Although I am angry with my brother, and I have not forgiven him – I may never forgive him – I will not lose another person today. Would Your Majesty entrust the imprisonment and punishment of Magnus Grey to me?"

The Seal-King regarded Dorian for a moment, and then conferred in whispers with other selkies on the council.

"I am told that you are trustworthy," said the Seal-King, "and have made a name for yourself as a detective, along with your human partner Leah Bishop. Is this true?"

Dorian lowered his gaze.

"I fear, Your Majesty, that Leah deserves most of the credit. As a detective, I..."

Here, Dorian paused, unsure of how to continue.

"I have made choices I regret."

The Seal-King observed him for some minutes, while the other selkies whispered amongst themselves.

"In itself, a worthy response," his low voice boomed across the cavernous space. "Can you guarantee his imprisonment? The new monster Sebastian is said to have escaped."

"Yes," Dorian agreed, "from the Deeps. No prisoner has escaped from there."

The Seal-King conferred in murmurs again with the council. He turned to Dorian with a slight nod.

"Very well," he said. "The court will agree on one condition."

"And that is?" asked Dorian.

"An appropriate punishment must be found," said the Seal-King. "I am not convinced that Magnus Grey truly repents of his crimes.

"These small human lives, so easily extinguished, are lost forever. The resulting pain and insanity of the Taken selk, as well as the creation of a monster like Sebastian, deserves a severe reprimand – a lasting one. A fitting punishment will be one that teaches Magnus Grey the value of a life, and the value of sacrifice. Can you guarantee this?"

Dorian bowed deeply.

"I give you my word."

"You have a month to discover the punishment," said the Seal-King. "If you do not, you will join your brother here in Faerie as prisoner."

"Understood."

The Seal-King addressed the court.

"Let my judgement be heard," said the Seal-King. "Magnus Grey will be confined in the Deeps of Caledonia Interpol until such time as his brother, Dorian Grey, who takes full responsibility for him, can discover a fitting punishment, or the brothers will share the same sentence.

"If all present are willing to accept this outcome, say aye."

The entire court replied with a unanimous *aye*. Dorian nodded his thanks, and did not show his concern beneath his confidence.

***

The fire was crackling merrily in the little stove in Gregoire's cave. He hummed to himself as he made tea.

Dorian entered, looking downtrodden. Gregoire nodded to him.

"She's awake now," he said, "you can talk."

"Hello, Miss Bishop," said Dorian.

Leah looked up at him, smiling weakly.

"You look like you've done something stupid," Leah said.

"I did what was right," said Dorian. "He is my brother."

"So what did you do?" asked Leah.

"I offered to take him back to Glasgow, to put him in the Deeps," he said.

"Good so far," said Leah.

"And the Seal-King agreed, but I have to find a suitable punishment for him that the council will agree on, or I will be given the same punishment as he has," said Dorian, "Which was death by overdose."

"*Dorian*," said Leah.

"You told me I needed to help him!" said Dorian.

"Not to the point of suicide!" said Leah. She shook her head.

"Gregoire, please tell my partner he is an idiot," said Leah. Gregoire hid a grin behind his teacup.

Dorian sighed.

"I need to return to Glasgow with Magnus," he said. Leah made a motion to stand, but he put out a hand to stop her. "Alone. We can't risk moving you."

"Dorian..." Leah began, but Dorian abruptly turned and walked away down the cave.

Gregoire brought her a cup of tea, smiling as he sat down beside her.

"Don't worry about him, Leah. He cares. He is a different man than I knew."

Leah accepted the tea, and took a sip.

"What was he like, back then?" she asked, to get her mind off her anger.

Gregoire smiled again.

"You wouldn't recognise him."

CHAPTER EIGHT

LONDON, ENGLAND
1890

The apartments rented by Dorian and Magnus Grey are nothing short of opulent. Dorian has been torn apart again and again in the press for his scandalous behaviour, at which he laughs, cuts out the articles, and tapes them to a board in the kitchen where the maids can read all about him.

This afternoon, he is otherwise occupied.

Magnus walked through door without knocking. Dorian was underneath the blankets, giggling.

"Dorian, it's time to leave."

Dorian sat up in bed, his long, beautiful black hair dishevelled. Another young man sat up beside him. Dorian gave his brother a look of annoyance.

"What is it?" Dorian demanded. "Can't you see I'm busy?"

"We are expected at the salon in an hour. If you could see fit to clothe yourself…"

Magnus covered his eyes out of politeness.

Dorian shook his head, and pulled the covers over himself and his companion. Magnus sighed and left the room.

The salon was crowded and stuffy. Magnus sat with Dorian, who was quite listless and clearly hungover. Magnus looked at him and shook his head.

"Ugh, why did you drag me out of bed for this?" Dorian asked. "These people are dull. They make me itch."

"You're drunk, Dorian," said Magnus. "You must be patient. Do you not wish to be present for such a historic day?"

"History can go hang," Dorian said. "I feel that you are altogether too scholarly, brother."

"There is nothing left for us now in the Highlands," said Magnus. "It is empty. Our people starve, Dorian."

"Again with our people," said Dorian. "Our people are the selkies, Magnus. We are not human. We don't owe allegiance to any people."

"If it weren't for the Highlanders, we would not have existed for the last several centuries," said Magnus. "You really ought to be more responsible, Dorian."

"Thank you. I will take that under advisement," said Dorian.

He banged his stick against the ground.

"Waiter! Champagne! What's taking so long?" he shouted. He turned to Magnus.

"Why do we not go somewhere more entertaining?" he asked. "Rome, or Paris – or Venice? Carnivale must have started, or will start soon."

"You really are an obnoxious boor," said Magnus. "We can visit those places later."

"Very well, if you say so," said Dorian, "but the lack of beautiful men or women in this club is vaguely alarming. Let us rectify this situation."

"No sooner said than done."

***

The brothers were seated in a cabaret, much darker than the salon, and a place of ill repute. Opium was available, and the young men and women there were for sale.

Dorian planned to make the best of it.

"This is more like it," said Dorian, "It is so good to be at the centre of the Empire, rather than the outskirts of it."

"I don't know," said Magnus. "I prefer Scotland. Everyone here is so pretentious."

"Meaning you can't lord over them here as you do there?" laughed Dorian, already high. "Well, everyone either lives here, visits here, or wants to be here. London is the centre of the civilised world, Magnus. We're the lucky ones."

They became vaguely aware of someone standing over them. Magnus looked up.

"You could attempt to be less of a blight on society and try doing something with your endless lives," said a voice.

Dorian finally made an effort, and looked up to see a man in his mid-50s; an imposing figure with bright blue eyes.

"Pardon me," said Dorian, with the indignant air of an extremely drunk rich person, "but I don't think you know who we are."

"A pair of layabouts, I expect," said the man. "I'm Detective Inspector Benandonner, and I'd like the two of you to come with me."

"What? Why?" said Magnus. "We've done nothing wrong."

Benandonner took in their illicit surroundings and then looked at the brothers.

"I think I'll be the judge of that," said D.I. Benandonner.

***

The brothers sat down with Benandonner. He cracked open a bottle of champagne, much to Dorian's evident relief.

"We are infiltrating the military," said Benandonner. "This war has gone on for centuries. We need to stop the disease at its source."

Dorian was shocked, and then horrified.

"Are you offering us a *job*?" he said in disgust. "Work makes me break out in hives. I'll pass."

"Interpol has been around longer than any of us," said Benandonner. "If you care in any way for the humans or even the other monsters, we need you."

"Why us? We're selkies," said Magnus. "Why us? We're not men of war."

"Exactly," said Benandonner. "And you're from Scotland."

"So?" said Magnus.

"So," said Benandonner. "No one will suspect you."

"And why on earth should we agree to this?" asked Dorian. "We're rich. We have no reason to fight, or to work."

"Because if you don't, this will spell the end of us all," said Benandonner.

"Surely it can't be that serious?" asked Magnus. "Humans have been fighting, doing drugs, having wars, for centuries. They're still around."

"Exactly the reason this is so important," Benandonner said. "If this war goes on much longer, there won't be any of them left. The fighting needs to end, at **any cost**."

"Very well," said Magnus, "I'll join. And I'll answer for my brother."

"Good choice," said Benandonner. "I'll see you back in Glasgow next week."

Benandonner pushed away from the table and stood. Magnus turned to Dorian, who was spitting tacks in his indignant fury, so angry he was unable to speak.

"Oh don't give me that look, Dorian," said Magnus. "You need some structure in your life and I will not watch as you destroy everything and everyone around you with your continued debauchery. Who knows? You may even enjoy it."

***

Dorian Grey didn't care about anything.

Or more precisely, he didn't care about any*one*.

He certainly cared about champagne and whisky, sumptuous feasts, and rolling with pretty boys and girls on the finest linen from Edinburgh to Rome.

His sincere belief was that his magic existed to cure hangovers, to impress his lovers, to charm his way onto steamships heading to exotic destinations. His life was filled with new intoxicating herbs and beautiful humans who would fall, by ones and twos, and even threes and fours, onto the silk sheets of his bed.

For Dorian Grey, immortal life was an endless carnival of bright colours, beautiful sighs, and vivid dreams.

For Dorian Grey, immortal life was all about *him*.

Magnus Grey, his older brother, was the fixed point that Dorian orbited like a ship at anchor. Magnus took care of the money, the chores, and the practical aspects of living. Dorian took care of the rest. He did not give his brother much thought, and only spoke with him when his funds were running low or he'd gotten himself into a sticky situation with a husband or wife that he needed Magnus's deft skill and soft voice to wheedle him out of.

There was not a pub, an opium den, or a brothel that Dorian did not know. His choices were highbrow, his taste impeccable; he only kissed the beautiful, he only ate or drank or smoked or injected what was expensive and came in tiny snuffboxes like treasure chests of gold.

One night, in the rich red-mirrored room of a London salon, in his drunken, drugged-out opium haze, Dorian fell in love.

He was walking the streets of London, laughing into the darkness, his cane clacking against the cobbles. He was alone, but he knew he wouldn't be for long. Men like Dorian never were – young, beautiful, well dressed, rich. A *comtesse* from the Continent? A handsome young protege, looking for that boost to help him in his political aspirations? There was no end to the possibility of the rich and varied London population, and it made Dorian's already endless hunger insatiable.

"Sir," said a voice at his right, an Irish voice, just as he was about to turn up the staircase to the salon.

Dorian sighed and gritted his teeth, continued walking.

"Please, sir," the voice said, "I'm very hungry."

There was a note of music in the voice. Against his better judgement, Dorian turned.

A beautiful young man, covered in the dirt and grime of London's underbelly, stared up at him with huge brown eyes. Dorian's breath hitched. A human, so like the selk. A filthy, starving human endowed with the same beauty as his own kind. Some deep part of him, some part connected to his ancient people, sang with near homesickness at the sight of this creature of his kind of beauty buried in mud.

Dorian looked at the young man's hopeful face, his jacket and clothing in tatters, and that deep part of him *pushed*.

Dorian offered the young man his hand.

"Come with me," he said, startling himself. "What's your name?"

The young man stared at him, as if he did dared not hope. He cautiously put his hand in Dorian's.

"Aidan."

***

The soft smile on Dorian's face was an unfamiliar sight to all who knew him. He watched Aidan with fondness.

Aidan was in his early 20s, and a recent arrival in the city. He had spent most of his life on a farm in rural Ireland and had spent the last of his wages to gain passage to London. He was provincial and needed tutelage, instruction in the fashion of the day, and training in comportment if he were to succeed in the city.

The young man had been cleaned up and dressed in proper attire. He was breathtakingly handsome, his huge dark eyes striking a painful chord of nostalgia in Dorian, reminding him of the selk and the value they placed on hearth and home. It was a value that he himself had rejected.

Dorian had ignored the Call, when it had come for him. He felt its pull, even now. Staring at Aidan, the guilt washed over him because he could still sense it: a wave kept from the shore, always searching.

"Thank you, sir," said Aidan. He sat in front of a feast in the red room with the mirrors, partridge and roast goose, all kinds of gravy, roast potatoes, wine and champagne. He had wolfed down what he could and Dorian had to stop him before Aidan made himself sick. He was currently seated in front of the largest piece of chocolate cake Dorian had ever seen, and his boyish grin warmed a part of the selkie's soul that he hadn't been aware of before.

"What have you come to London to do?" Dorian asked.

The young man swallowed his bite of cake before responding. Manners had been taught, Dorian noted; this was a good thing.

"I want to be a dancer, sir," said Aidan. "I want to join the ballet."

Dorian grinned at that; he loved talent, and appreciated the fine musculature of dancers, as well as the brutal regime that kept them in training.

"Please, don't call me sir," he said. "My name is Dorian. I'll see what I can do for you, if you are talented enough."

Aidan smiled, and Dorian knew his heart would never be the same.

***

In the weeks to come, and the months to follow, their relationship went from artist and sponsor to an entirely different one. Dorian had made the proper introductions, and had intended to leave Aidan alone to succeed or fail. He did not want a relationship with a young man who felt he owed the selkie anything, and in all other *liaisons* Dorian would have enjoyed a night with a beautiful body and said his farewells. This time was different; Dorian *wanted* him, heart and soul.

So Dorian walked away.

He woke, head pounding with the combination cocktail he'd administered himself the night before, to forget Aidan's huge eyes and the way he laughed. The bell was ringing, loudly against the door, jangling as someone pulled hard on it. Dorian groaned and wrapped himself in his dressing gown, pushing a bit of his magic through the headache so he could at least communicate with whoever was waiting outside.

He opened the door and there were those large eyes staring up at him, full of tears.

Aidan stood on the stoop, twisting his hat in his hands.

"Forgive me for coming here, Dorian," said Aidan. "What have I done to displease you?"

Dorian blinked.

"Displease…?" he began. "You have done nothing to displease me, Aidan."

"Then why did you stop speaking to me?!" Aidan said, "I waited, after the performance, and you were not in your box and I haven't seen you in a week."

Dorian sighed, and rubbed his eyes.

"Aidan," he said, and how difficult was a confession for this man who had never loved, "I…did not want to be inappropriate, as my affections for you were not what they should have been."

A light in Aidan's eyes made Dorian hope, and hate himself for it.

"Affections?" Aidan asked.

Dorian nodded, and was startled by the press of Aidan's lips against his own.

"I have loved you," said Aidan, murmuring between kisses, "since the night I saw you."

***

Aidan slept against Dorian's shoulder. The selkie absently touched the curls at the top of his lover's head, and Aidan made a noise in his sleep, curling in and burying his face in Dorian's long, black hair.

Love

said the Call, speaking to him, deep and certain.

This is what waits for you. This is your purpose, your destiny.

You have left it too long, Dorian Grey.

Magic has its purpose.

Don't I have a choice? Dorian wondered, sending the question into the ether, *I choose him. Always.*

Before the Call, you had a choice, the seals murmured to him, *you are beholden, betrothed to another.*

Dorian sighed. He felt it, the Call, pulling him, calling to him, relentless as the waves upon the sea. He stared down at Aidan, loved and lover.

Dorian hoped he would remember him, afterwards.

CHAPTER NINE

CALEDONIA INTERPOL

Magnus was shoved into a cell in the Caledonia Interpol Deeps, and he turned as the lock slid home behind him. He saw Dorian standing there, silent.

"Dorian…" he began.

"Don't. Just don't," said Dorian. "I had to come back to Glasgow because of you. If I lose Leah…"

"Still," said Magnus. "Thank you, brother."

But Dorian was already walking up the stairs.

Magnus sighed to himself. He lay down across the bench and was soon asleep.

After some time, he sensed a presence in the cell, and he stirred. He opened his eyes with a start.

A woman stood next to him, watching.

Magnus stared at her.

"Hazel?"

***

The commotion in the Deeps could be heard throughout Caledonia Interpol. Chief Ben, Dorian, and Yoo Min rushed down the stairs. As they rounded the corner, the words of the argument became clearer.

"You killed me, you bastard!"

"And I'm in prison! I'm paying for it!"

*"I'm **dead**!"*

The three newcomers stared at the scene in disbelief. Magnus sat placidly next to Hazel, who was fading in and out of existence. She was still beautiful, her hair piled in a perfect late '60s style beehive, sunglasses perched on her head, white gloves and a Mod dress with white gogo boots. In her life, Hazel had been a talented fashion designer, her clothes popular with the jet set and everybody who was anybody in Swinging London.

She stared at Magnus, her arms crossed. Yoo Min glared at them while Ben and Dorian stared.

"Who is this woman, *sunbae*?" Yoo Min snarled. "Your brother's liver is **mine**!"

"It's Hazel," said Dorian, unable to believe his own eyes. "It's *Hazel Bloodworth*."

"Who?" asked Yoo Min.

"Dorian!" said Magnus, catching sight of them. "Thank goodness you're here, she won't go away. Can't you get rid of her?"

Hazel crossed her arms.

"Don't you *dare*, Dorian Grey."

"It's good to see you again, Hazel," said Dorian.

"I can't say the same," said Hazel crossly, and then relented, "Oh, Dorian, I'm glad to see you, of course, but...why am I here?"

"It's not the cell, if that's what you're asking," said a voice. Milo rolled forward in his wheelchair.

"How do you mean?" asked Magnus.

"Well, you see, I have been studying it since the phenomena first appeared about a week ago," Milo explained.

"A *week* ago?" asked Benandonner. "You knew about this? And you said nothing about it?"

Milo shot him an indignant look.

"You've never shown much interest in my research," he said reproachfully.

"This one is *mine*, Milo, I have marked him!" insisted Yoo Min.

Milo stared at Yoo Min, unimpressed.

"You can have him," said Milo dryly. "I don't like selkie. Too salty. Anyway, this phenomenon began to appear around a week ago – "

Hazel stamped her foot.

"I am *not* a phenomenon!" she said.

For some reason, Magnus decided this was the time to turn on the charm.

"I always thought so," he said with a lazy smile.

"Really, Magnus?!" said Hazel. "Really?! **Now?**"

"Too soon?" asked Magnus.

Milo cleared his throat.

"As I was saying, Hazel first appeared about a week ago," he said. "It's not the anniversary of anything, or related to current events. In fact, I cannot tell why she has manifested – and neither can she."

"You've been talking to each other all this time?" asked Chief Ben.

"Oh, yes," said Hazel. "Milo has been very kind and supportive."

"*Slut*," muttered Magnus under his breath.

"What did you just call me, Magnus Grey?!" Hazel demanded.

"*Quiet, everyone!*" said Dorian. He nodded politely at Milo.

"Yes, thank you, Dorian," said Milo. "In my research, I have discovered that she isn't haunting the cell, but him."

"Him? What do you mean?" asked Yoo Min.

"She's haunting *him*," Milo clarified. "Not the cell, or the prison, or the Interpol station. She's haunting Magnus Grey."

Hazel's mouth dropped open. Magnus went white.

"You mean to tell me that I'm stuck with him?" Hazel demanded.

"Until we find out what's happened, it seems that way," said Milo.

"This must be some trick! A punishment! A curse, or a spell!" said Magnus. "Dorian, you can't let this happen!"

Dorian stared at his brother.

"If you can give Hazel her life back, I will help you," he said. "If you can bring back the humans you have murdered, I will help you. I only continue to call you *brother* because I must."

Dorian turned on his heel and walked out, Magnus staring after him. Chief Ben nodded to the group.

"I'll go talk to him," said Ben. "You think you can handle this one on your own, Yoo Min?"

The Korean woman smiled at him.

"I'm thousands of years older than you, Ben," she said sweetly. "I think I'll be fine."

"Good," said Ben, who was quite happy to follow Dorian up the stairs. Much as he didn't like to admit it, the gumiho unnerved him more than any monster he'd encountered in many years.

Yoo Min approached the cell.

"Hi, Hazel," she said. "I'm Detective Inspector Lee Yoo Min."

Hazel was looking up at the ceiling, trying not to cry. She slowly looked down at the other woman. Yoo Min smiled winsomely. She had settled down now that it was clear Hazel wouldn't be getting in the way of her designs on the selkie.

"Can you tell me what's happened to Sebastian?" asked Hazel. "My poor, sweet husband, he must have suffered so much!"

"Yes, what a smashing success!" said Magnus bitterly. "What a great man he was, how sweet and innocent! Poor, sweet Sebastian became the head of the greatest crime syndicate Glasgow has ever known! He's so clever even Leah and Dorian can't find him."

"*You shut your mouth!*" snarled Hazel. "How dare you accuse Sebastian of something so horrible? I didn't ask you!"

Hazel looked imploringly at Yoo Min, who stared at the floor.

"Is it true?" asked Hazel. "Yoo Min, is it true? Tell me it's not true."

"Yes," said Yoo Min. "It's all true. I was briefed on it when I arrived. It was your murder that started everything."

"So Magnus started it all," murmured Hazel. Magnus turned to look at the two women.

"Well, I couldn't have known," he said. "Who could've predicted such a milquetoast would become so powerful."

"I knew," said Hazel. The other two looked at her in surprise.

"Not that he would turn out this way," Hazel explained hastily, "but that he had more potential, more strength, more – everything, than you ever took the time to know, Magnus. He called you his best friend, but you only hung around with him because you pitied him. I understand now. Death gives you perspective, and time to think."

"He was never good enough for you, Hazel," said Magnus, "and now he's an infamous criminal. I would have saved you from the indignity that –"

"I was perfectly capable of making my own choices, then and now," said Hazel. "You view everything as a possession, something to covet. Something to *steal*. I know what you did to me, Magnus. You're not the better man here."

"Excuse me?!" cried Magnus.

"You're in the strongest prison that Caledonia Interpol has available," said Hazel, "and Sebastian is walking free. So either he's not as evil, or he's smarter. Either way, he's a better man than you, even if he *is* a criminal."

"How do you *know* all this?" asked Magnus. "I never told you about this other world, or – or what I really am."

"There's more to me than meets the eye, Magnus Grey," she said. "You just never saw it, because you can't see past your own ego. And what you really are, is evil. Beautiful or not, selkie or not, you're the kind of monster that's the reason for monster stories."

Magnus was stunned into silence.

Yoo Min decided to break it.

"Sebastian's still out there, somewhere," she confirmed. "But your appearance now is a strange coincidence. We've got other problems."

Hazel turned away from where Magnus was slowly boiling over.

"How do you mean?" she asked.

"Well, how much do you know about Caledonia Interpol? The Fae?" asked Yoo Min.

Hazel grinned, a mysterious glint in her eye.

"Let's say, more than you think, and much more than Magnus would believe. I am, after all, just a human woman."

She winked, and Yoo Min thought she rather liked this woman.

"A while ago, one of the city's Guardians found a woman dying in a Bridgeton close," said Yoo Min. "Her hands were blackened."

Hazel stared at the gumiho.

"Blackened?" she asked. "Like a plague victim's?"

"Exactly like that," said Yoo Min. "Right now, we are investigating why the Black Death has returned to Glasgow. We don't have much time."

Hazel turned paler, if that were possible.

"The Black Death?!" she said.

"Yes," said Yoo Min, "or something very like it. Glasgow has been quarantined. We are losing the humans rapidly. We think that while the disease is natural in itself, it is magical in origin. According to Dorian, we know the source but not the cure, unless the particular strain is discovered, or the cause is isolated. No doctor has been able to stop it. Humans are falling ill at a rapid pace, and we are at a loss."

Hazel stood, lost in thought, for some time.

"I could help," she said eventually.

"How?" asked Yoo Min. "Were you a doctor?"

"I thought about training to be one, if I gave up fashion," said Hazel. "I was a witch."

There was stunned silence, and something like fear permeated the air. Yoo Min took a step back. Magnus looked at Hazel in horror.

"How could you not tell me?" he demanded. "You were a *witch* and you didn't tell me!"

"It's a good thing I didn't, or else I'd have truly been enslaved to you," said Hazel. "You're not a very nice person, Magnus."

"But how could you help us?" asked Yoo Min.

"Because that's what witches do," said Hazel. "One of the things, anyway, despite our bad reputation both with humans and the Fae. But if I were going to help, I'd have to be out in the city, not in the Deeps. There's far too much dampening of magic down here for me to do anything useful. My compliments to the architect, but I'm not much use to you stuck in prison with my own murderer."

"Yes, Magnus would have to accompany her, if she were to go outside," Milo said suddenly. Everyone jumped; they had quite forgotten the merman was there. Fading easily into the background was a part of his own magic, but he still gave them an annoyed look as if they had been ignoring him on purpose. "There would be no other way, as the situation stands. Unfortunately, Hazel is moored to him for some reason. I am still investigating a way to break this tie, but I haven't found it yet."

Magnus began to grin in a very unsettling way. He clearly saw a path to freedom opening up in front of him.

"I wouldn't be so smug," said Milo. "Hazel will be in charge, if this is approved, and you're tethered whether you like it or not. You wanted her to be your wife, well, now you have the opportunity of being with her 24/7."

Milo turned to Hazel. His expression softened in a way that would surprise anyone who had known the merman. He wasn't known for his sympathetic nature or gentleness, but something about Hazel seemed to bring it out in him.

"I am sorry about this, and about the situation you're in," he said gently. "We will work on a solution, but we are running out of time."

Hazel nodded, and took Milo's hand, much to Magnus's dismay.

"I understand," she said. "Maybe was the reason I was brought back. What other reason could there be?"

***

Some hours later, Milo was alone in the lab again, industriously working on a way to separate Hazel from Magnus. He sat with an enormous tome in his lap, paging through various spells and images from throughout the centuries.

The lab was bright and welcoming, despite the things that tended to go on in there. Milo's experiments were less than savoury and he skirted the line of black magic enough that if it weren't for his brilliance and his dedication to Interpol, he might've found himself on the opposite side of the bars.

The lab could only be accessed through the Labyrinth beneath the station, so Milo did not often receive visitors. Since Milo's lab also contained the morgue, also for questionable reasons it was probably best not to look too closely at, his visitors were usually police officers.

Dorian pushed the door open to see Milo bent over a book, his orange tail draped in a bucket of water. At the sound of the door closing, the *ceasg* looked up and pushed his glasses higher on his nose.

"Oh, thank God," said Milo. "Hello again, Dorian. Good timing. I could use the interruption."

Dorian crouched beside Milo in a strange manner peculiar to the selk.

"What can you tell me about witches?" he asked.

Milo moved a few of the beakers on the desk, and peered into a microscope.

"Is this about Hazel?" he asked mildly, not looking at the detective.

"Yes," said Dorian. "I don't understand why you didn't tell us about this sooner, Milo."

The merman sighed. His orange tail splashed water as he turned to pick up a petri dish.

"I enjoyed having company," said Milo. "It's been rather quiet down here, since Geoffrey left."

He looked around the large, cavernous space.

"Your prejudices are quite clear," Milo continued. "I wasn't willing to share, just yet."

"Hazel is an old friend," said Dorian. "Whatever prejudices I have, I'd have liked to know."

"Then why are you here asking me if witches are dangerous, instead of asking after her well-being?" asked Milo. "It's clear to me you're here in your capacity of detective. You and the others also seem to like me for my usefulness but not for my nature. It's as if you draw a line between monsters, when that's what all of us are."

Dorian watched Milo work for a while in silence. He wasn't certain what to say, primarily because he felt in his bones that Milo was probably right.

"My apologies, Milo," he finally chose to say. "You're absolutely right. I shall endeavour to do better in the future, and not let prejudice cloud my judgement. It seems no matter how old we are, some of us are still learning."

"Some of you, indeed," sniffed Milo. "The rest of you don't use your age to gain wisdom or to change your ways, but to plough the furrow of prejudice even deeper."

Milo began moving some items around on the table in front of him. It seemed like he was off in his own world, so Dorian waited patiently. Eventually, the merman spoke again. It almost seemed as if he were doing it against his better judgement.

"Long ago, witches were feared, by kings and by the kind of people who were interested in burning other people at the stake," he said. "Most of the time, they work with herbs and help women with their health. Why do you ask?"

"Are they evil? Inherently?" Dorian pressed. Milo all but rolled his eyes.

"How do you not know the answer to this question, Dorian?" asked Milo. "You've been alive for a very long time."

"I wasn't exactly paying attention for most of it," said Dorian. "Other things to do."

"Other things, I see," said Milo, whose tone of voice said he knew exactly what those other things were.

"Milo," said Dorian, reminding him of the topic at hand.

"No, of course they're not inherently evil," sighed Milo, "and especially not if this question is about Hazel. I think the problem, you will find, is not that witches are evil. It's that they are too good."

Dorian looked puzzled.

"We're *monsters*, Dorian," said Milo. "As I mentioned before. Technically, *I* am inherently evil. In general, every one of us is a monster, in the classic sense of the word. We're just reformed. Witches are *human*. That means that they have chosen to learn magic, and have entered this world of their own volition. It's not natural to them; they aren't born with it, as we are. But a human does not depend on draining others in order to survive. A human can exist without draining a soul, like a merman; drinking blood, like a vampire; or even – yes – living off love, like a selkie."

"Some people might call that survival," said Dorian.

"They might," said Milo. "I call it addiction. Apart from specific monsters, like your new gumiho officer, most of us can survive without the element we drain. We're immortal, so it might be uncomfortable, but we don't *need* to do it. We choose to do it. This is evident in the ability of many of the Fae to change their ways or to drink blood from other sources, take souls from creatures other than human.

"No, Dorian. We don't need any of it to survive. We demand it because we think it's our *right*. We're addicts, my friend, as much as any Fae who loved the Smoke. We love to gorge ourselves. We are creatures of pleasure, Dorian, not survival.

"Everyone here – *everyone* – is an alcoholic, one drink shy of falling off the wagon."

***

The day was calm and still. Not even a soft wind ruffled the water of the river. The streets were empty of people. They hadn't seen one other living person on their walk from the station at St. Enoch to the water's edge.

Seagulls wheeled in the air above the Clyde, apparently unaffected by the plague. They were the only living things left in this place, and the experience was sobering. Although it had been some time since Magnus was out and about in Glasgow, he had never seen the place so deathly quiet.

Yoo Min sat beside Magnus on a bench next to the river. They didn't speak to each other, just breathed the air together underneath the slate-grey sky. He smiled, happy to be outside once again despite the situation.

A woman flashed into existence beside them, looking irritated.

"Let's go, Magnus," said Hazel.

His reverie was shattered. He glared at the woman he had once loved beyond reason.

"None of that," said Hazel. "I'd leave you here alone in a second if I could, you know that. We have to go. We're expected."

Grumbling, Magnus stood up and walked along the canal, Yoo Min following silently like an animal hunting, tailing its victim through the woods. In the distance, they could make out three figures silhouetted in the greylight of the Glasgow sky.

Magnus and Yoo Min walked to the wharf where Dorian, Ben, and Milo were waiting. Hazel blinked into existence again beside them. Milo was on the ground in classic mermaid pose beside his wheelchair, his bright orange tail shimmering in the light like goldfish scales. His lab coat draped around his slender, muscular upper body, his skin burnished green and gold to match. He was studying a body lying on the path with interest.

"What are you doing out with your tail uncovered, Milo?" Yoo Min asked after a while. "Aren't you worried someone is going to see you?"

"There aren't many humans around," Milo replied, gesturing to indicate the general absence of people in the area without looking up. "Everyone is afraid – and rightly so. I doubt there's much risk."

A woman walking along the canal with shopping bags in her hands dropped them. She stared at the group for a moment, then turned and ran back along the river's edge.

"All right, maybe *some* risk," muttered Milo. "Not sure if that was brave or stupid of her. Or me. Either way, the humans are terrified. They're staying confined to their houses, for the most part."

"What about her groceries?" asked Hazel. "She'll need those one way or the other."

"One of the pixies will deliver them," said Chief Ben, already on the phone to Aoife. "No need to make things worse."

"Why *aren't* things worse, Chief?" asked Dorian. "I'd have expected outright panic by now. Looting. Riots in the streets. *Something.*"

"Humans are a funny breed," said Ben. "Sometimes they run. Sometimes they fight. Sometimes they freeze. They haven't seen a disaster of this kind, on this scale, in centuries. Not in this part of the world, anyway. They're not used to a daily understanding of their own mortality. Frankly, neither are we. Not anymore."

"I have to say, it's upsetting even me," said Milo. "I'm not accustomed to the idea of not knowing the answer."

"Arrogance," said Magnus, who knew that failing all too well.

"No, Magnus," said Milo. "*You're* arrogant. In my case, it's just fact. I am rather brilliant, you know."

Magnus' incredulous look was sure to be followed by something stupid, so Hazel stepped in.

"So what can you tell us about the body?" she asked.

"Another collapse," said Milo, already absorbed in the mystery again. "Humans are dying all over the city. Seems to last for around two weeks, and that's it. We're not sure whether –"

The corpse groaned.

"This person isn't dead yet," Hazel pointed out helpfully.

"Not yet," said Milo. "He will be soon."

"What are we doing here, watching someone die?" asked Dorian. "You have strange ideas, Milo."

"There's nothing we can do for him," said Milo, ever the pragmatist. "I want to see if he manifests as a ghost."

"You want to fill us in here?" asked Ben.

Milo scratched the back of his head with his pen.

"Ghosts," he murmured to himself, as if no one else was there. "It's not about the plague. Or the Smoke. It's about ghosts. I think Hazel haunting Magnus is unrelated to the illness, but I had to bring him here to be sure. Now I'm certain. This has something to do with Magnus alone."

"Why would that be?" asked Dorian.

"Punishment?" Milo offered.

"But didn't Magnus kill a lot of people? Wouldn't that mean –" Yoo Min began, and her voice died in her throat.

Magnus looked around in horror. A blonde woman covered in blood was glaring at him from a doorway, with her arms crossed. Further away, down the river, another woman stood on the quay. A young man in a beret sat staring at him in accusation. Two more young men seated on the steps nearby turned to look at him.

Magnus went white.

"There are so many of them!" cried Magnus. Hazel raised an eyebrow.

"We have to sort this out! I mean –" he said.

"How many people did you murder, brother?" interrupted Dorian softly.

"But...all these people!!!" Magnus said. "You can't let them do this! It's torture!"

The old giant stared at Magnus, and said nothing.

***

The clouds parted above Caledonia Interpol's library. The fire roared in the fireplace as Dorian walked into the office. He sat down on the antique sofa and looked at the empty seat usually occupied by his partner. Leah'd be hungover as usual and giving him the evil eye over his newspaper. Then she'd crack a lewd joke he would never admit he found funny. He sighed. He missed her, and hoped Gregoire and Robert were looking after her.

Out of the corner of his eye, he noticed his brother was sitting at the desk nearby, talking with Yoo Min. He was still surrounded by various bloody ghosts. His hair was dishevelled and he looked a mess. It seemed like there were new ghosts now. Caledonia Interpol may have been large enough to generate its own weather, but the place was starting to feel rather crowded.

Dorian stood from the sofa and went to his desk. He ignored Magnus, although he could feel the selkie's eyes on him.

"Why won't you look at me, brother?" Magnus said.

Dorian rifled through the papers on his desk with impatience. He really needed to get back to the Highlands, and Leah.

"I don't know who you are speaking to, using that word," murmured Dorian.

"I am suffering, Dorian!" Magnus said, in anguish. "These ghosts, they won't leave me alone –"

*"Then **suffer**, Magnus Grey!"* Dorian shouted, startling everyone, including himself.

Magnus stared open mouthed at his brother's back as Dorian retreated into the distance. He couldn't even catch the eye of the other officers. Suddenly he was aware of someone on his left, and he looked into the worshipful eyes of Yoo Min. She smiled slowly.

"You wouldn't mind terribly, would you, if I ate your liver?" she asked sweetly.

CHAPTER TEN

CESSNOCK BANKS
THE LAND OF THE FAE

The Cessnock Water was once a beautiful, secluded river, its water running clear. For the humans, it still did. For the Fae, it seemed as though it never would again.

There wasn't much desirable about war. The air was filled with smoke, the tents along the riverside stuffy, and their inhabitants too wary to risk themselves out in the water for a bath, because it made them vulnerable. This particular war, and its soldiers, were hidden from most human eyes, apart from those who could see in other ways, by scrying glass or crystal ball. Some humans were born with an innate ability to see their world, but they were extremely rare.

Robert Burns turned out to be just such a human, much to Desdemona's chagrin.

The camp of the Fae battalion was on Cessnock Banks, where she had set up her tent. Her soldiers followed suit, and so they made up a sort of village at the water's edge. Fortunately, the trees hid them from the surrounding fields, and the dun colour of the tents hid them from prying enemy eyes.

Disregarding any need for invitation or announcing himself, Robert approached Desdemona's tent and pushed open the flap.

Desdemona was seated on a small stool, alone, stitching up a wound in her arm by candlelight. She looked up, startled, only to be confronted with Robert's big, sad eyes.

"What are you doing here, Robert?!" she hissed. Robert did not reply, only watched her pull the thread through her wound, and then looked away.

"I had to see if you were all right," he mumbled.

"How the hell did you get past the sentries?" she demanded. "Even Iain?! How did you even *find* this place?"

Robert gave her a troubled look.

"I had to see if you were all right," he repeated, a helpless look in his eyes.

Desdemona barked a humourless laugh.

"I'm a vampire, Robert Burns," she said. "I'll survive. I *always* survive."

Explosions thudded dully around the tent. Desdemona stared at Robert, as if trying to puzzle him out. Robert sat down beside her. She looked very tired.

"You're telling me that you could see the camp just because you *wanted* to?" she asked.

Robert shrugged.

"I wanted to see *you*," he clarified. Her green eyes sparked, a strange fire, and she dropped that line of questioning.

"What's it like out there?" she grit out.

Robert shook his head.

"It's not going well," he replied.

Desdemona nodded, tightening the thread she had sewn through her wound with her teeth. Robert gently took her arm, and turned her toward him. She stared at him with suspicion until he tied the thread off for her.

"Thank you," she said gruffly. She sat back and stared at the ceiling. "All this, just for the Smoke. I should've stuck to whisky."

Robert shouted a laugh, more an expression of stress than anything. He nodded.

"Fae Wars," he said. "Had I known –"

He was interrupted by a loud explosion. Robert looked up, as a bomb rattled the earth and dust fell. Desdemona shook

114

the dust from her hair with the kind of nonchalance bred of familiarity.

"We are as unreasoning as humans, in some ways," she said.

Robert turned to her.

"Desdemona, I..."

She shook her head, smiling. The pain bothered her, a little.

"Save it," she said. "Don't you start that, Robert Burns. You poets are all the same."

Robert looked at her desperately.

"But I love –"

She held up a hand.

"You love every woman you come across," she said. "If you want to do me a favour, get back out there and save those stupid new recruits. They are in over their heads."

"I might die!" Robert said, emotion getting the better of him. "You forget, I am mortal."

"And you forget," she said, "that I am not."

She stood, and left the tent.

***

The forest around the Cessnock Water was deep and gloomy, even at midday. Desdemona liked to walk among the trees, as they offered some shelter from the sunlight, and respite from what sometimes seemed like a never-ending war.

As she walked in the soft dusk of the forest, she sensed that someone was following her. She halted on the path.

"Robert," she guessed easily. "What are you doing?"

She turned around to face him.

Robert looked at her, and then at the moon, hanging white and silver in the sky.

"I need you to make me one of you," he said. "And you're the only one who can."

Desdemona laughed.

"You're an idiot," she said. "Anyway, you'd make a better selkie. But no, Robert. We're doing this *for* you. For all humans."

"I have lived out my human life now, as you advised," he said. "I have had great success – fame, love, riches. And it has been a good life.

"I have done all you asked, and I have returned as I promised. Let me help you."

"This is self-sacrificing nonsense, Robert, you have plenty of time –"

"I'm sick, Desdemona. This whisky is going to be the death of me. Or the fever. The good doctor tells me I don't have much time left."

"We're defending your kind," Desdemona said. "It's been risky enough having you around as it is, but part of your blessing is that you're *mortal*. I'm not taking that away from you. You don't know what you're asking."

"Yes, I'm mortal," he said. "And I'm one of the only humans who is even aware of this war. I want to fight with you, Desdemona, and to do it without you having to protect me all the time. I need you to turn me into a vampire."

Desdemona felt her resolve beginning to weaken, before this strange young man who could apparently see Faerie just because he really wanted to check up on his crush. She paced back and forth, wondering if he didn't have some kind of magic of his own.

"I don't know if I can," she said. "Like I said, I've been *baobhan sith* for centuries, I was born *baobhan sith*. It's the only reality I've ever known. Besides, all *baobhan sith* are women. I don't even know if it would work on a man – and if it doesn't, then *I'll* have killed you. No thanks."

She turned away, and much to Desdemona's consternation, Robert fell to his knees behind her on the forest floor. He made quite the image, bowed in supplication in the thin shafts of sunlight drifting across the forest. Desdemona looked away, embarrassed for him and even more convinced there was something fey in him, after all.

"I know you don't believe in the love I have for you," he said, in a loud and clear voice filled with absolute conviction, "but it

116

is sincere, and it is all-consuming. I trust you, Desdemona, and I would rather fight than die by your side."

Desdemona looked at him. She felt herself pulled forward, almost as if it were not by her own design.

The *baobhan sith* approached Robert, who remained on his in deference to her, but his large, brilliant dark eyes stared up at her with something akin to worship. She touched his cheek, a caress that was almost loving. He pressed into it, eyes slowly closing in his ecstasy, as he savoured the first time the star of his heart touched him. She could taste his thoughts, now that they were close to each other, images scattered and tumbling through the void, stars and stardust, a chant against the beating of his heart

Love…love…she is…she is…want…

submit

The sexual imagery that followed this order confused her, as she grew her talons and her eyes flashed green, burying the sharp points deep in his neck til the blood throbbed out, coursing rivers down her nails, and she ran out her tongue for a taste. Her eyes rolled back in her head and she snarled; the mere taste of him had turned her feral, her eyes sudden bright green embers in the dark. She retracted her talons in one swift motion and closed her mouth over the pulsing wound, sucking hard at the life there. She wrapped herself around his body, and he let out a whine as she sat astride him, clinging to him in her hunger as it roared a waterfall in her head, and she could feel him, and the want in him, as he clutched at her and the sharp slant of his hipbones pushed against her in mindless want, now an urgent tattoo, and his fingertips dug into her skin as he filled the air with a piercing cry, his desire slaked as her thirst was…

She pushed him away suddenly, and he fell to the earth where she had found him. He looked up at her with amber eyes more reverent than before, blood still pulsing from the wound at his neck, his skin want-white, and she had to force herself to pull away from him, to stand up and turn around so she would no longer be tempted, to remove the scent of his blood from her nose so he would survive, the taste of his life was so sweet, so uniquely *him* that it had taken her breath away. She licked at the blood spread across her lips and face, and doubled over, nearly turning back to him with the want of it.

Images suddenly flooded her consciousness, unbidden and strange.

The future, fanned out like a deck of playing cards in her mind. His face, rendered in bronze, from Glasgow to Camperdown to Milwaukee.

There has been no man like him, nor will there be.

She found herself crouching near the ground, when she came to. She finally steeled herself to turn and look at him again. His amber eyes now glowed softly, lamps in the darkness much like her own. She tried to ignore the weak pulse of blood at his neck and remain aloof to the situation. She wondered how much of her own mind Robert could see. So far, his worshipful expression hadn't changed, so it appeared he did not have the power to taste minds quite yet. She felt bizarrely thankful for this, because she didn't understand the feelings coursing through her own body, as if she had taken a particularly wild and dangerous drug. *It's his blood in you,* she thought. She sat back on her heels, staring at him for a moment, before she opened her own wrist with a talon and let him drink his own blood from her veins, for she had none of her own.

She was reeling. She drank the blood of men every week. There should not have been anything particularly different this time.

Brusquely, she hauled Robert to his feet, and was a little rougher with him now, because this time it had been different. She had been a vampire for eons, further back than most could remember, and she had never experienced anything quite like their encounter on the soft pine needles of that forest floor.

"Come on," she said, wiping her mouth to rid herself of the last remnant of his blood. "Dawn's coming. Let's get you inside."

***

🌸 Chapter Ten 🌸

Once upon a time, there was a young boy in Seal-Hame.

There were shadows and secrets among the rocks, in the seaweed that undulated slowly through the underwater kingdom of the seals. This boy's birth had been the celebration and joy of every seal in Seal-Hame, and echoed throughout vast oceans, the silent heavy darkness of the deep.

For, among the beautiful, he was transcendent.

He was the most beautiful child recorded in all the history of Seal-Hame. There had been no other child like him before, not in all the years winding down into centuries, not in the blood memory of the people.

Iain Grey was the pride of the seal-folk.

He was unnaturally quiet. This concerned the Elders but they assigned his reticence to an introspective nature. He would be, they felt, the most successful of all selkies; an earnest and passionate lover, soft and gentle, strong and kind. The hopes and dreams of the selk rested on the boy.

He grew into a lithe young man, and was even more lovely than he had been as a child. He was impossible, and his clan boasted of him at every opportunity. As a seal, he was sleek and moved through the water like a current. In his human form, with his long, straight brown hair caressing a white and well-formed cheek, his black eyes captivated human and seal alike.

Iain Grey, beautiful and perfect prince of the seals, had a secret.

He longed for battle, and war.

Selkies, on the whole, were a peaceful race, content with flowing through the seabeds in the cold darkness of Seal-Hame. They dreamily composed poetry about their future loves, male or female; their hearts were easily excited and broken, their love of beauty famed.

Iain could not fall in love. He did not want that for himself. He could tell no one.

Once upon a time, a seal-boy strayed too far from the beach.

Iain walked in the forest, wondering at the strange cool feeling of the pine needles against his bare feet. The shadows of the pines played across his white and stately frame, as he walked staring up at the trees, and the sky, which seemed to him just another sea, blue and deep.

There was someone standing in the clearing ahead.

Curious, Iain approached. The sturdy figure turned, and he gasped at the green eyes, so striking to a boy who had seen only the dark eyes of the selk. The eyes were all he could focus on, for the moment, until the figure grinned. The white teeth startled him.

"Well," she said. "Not that I'm complaining, but where are your clothes?"

Iain stared at her, and then pointed behind himself, towards the sea.

"Selkie?" she asked. He nodded.

"You'd better get out of here," she said, "this is no place for one of you. The battle's over the hill but I think it might come to the edge of the water, foolish as that'd be. I'm scouting for the medic, he's going to need room for the wounded."

"You're a soldier?" the boy asked, startled at the sound of his disused voice. It was clear, and sweet, if rusty.

"More than that," said Desdemona, "I'm the commander of the army. I'm telling you, get out of here."

Iain looked toward the sea again, and home, and the endless litany of praise, of the hopes of his people.

"Can I join?" he asked. Desdemona's eyes narrowed, the green flash unmistakable.

"A selkie's got no business in this place," she said. "It is dark and violent and love is very far from here."

Iain nodded.

"Yes," he said. "I understand. Let me join. I cannot go back home."

"Why's that?" asked Desdemona.

Iain swallowed, nervous.

"I can't fall in love," he said, and it was something of a relief to say it aloud, after all this time. "And I don't want to."

"That's unusual for one of your kind," she said. She took out a long, slender white pipe and packed it with tobacco. Lighting it on fire, she took a long pull and breathed out a plume of smoke.

"I don't think it's ever happened before," said Iain. "Please, may I join you?"

Desdemona smoked for a while, lost in thought. For some reason, Iain's words seemed to weaken her resolve. She seemed to be thinking of something, a long-ago memory.

She sighed.

"All right," she said. "Is your sealskin hidden well enough? I'm not having you drawn off by someone. And you stay behind me or beside me at all times. I'm not going searching for you."

Iain nodded his agreement.

"What's your name?" she asked.

"Iain Grey," he replied.

"Well, Iain," she said, "much as it pains me, I think we need to get you some clothing."

**

The outcry when Iain disappeared was heartbreaking. The wailing shook the seabeds of Seal-Hame. It echoed in the sea-mounts, travelled via the whales and other voyagers across the oceans of the world.

He is lost, mourned the seals. *What a brief and dying spark is beauty. A star was extinguished tonight.*

The oceans wept, the creatures grieved for the sweet and innocent beauty captured or captivated, murdered by some crude and calloused hand.

In the forest, miles away, Iain Grey shouldered his rifle and fell into step behind Desdemona, the only woman he would follow for the rest of his days.

CALEDONIA INTERPOL

At Caledonia Interpol, the mist had rolled in, and gave the

library a hazy glow.

Magnus was backed against a wall of books, Yoo Min advancing on him.

"You see," she said, "you're not a human man. So if I ate your liver, it would grow back, and I would never have to be hungry again, and you would never have to be –"

Magnus felt around for the door handle and started to pull it open. Yoo Min slammed it shut.

"– alone."

Magnus stared at her and swallowed. He did not remember ever being so terrified.

"You do know..." he stuttered, "that I am – was – a murderer."

"Yes, *oppa*," she said. "So was I! But this way we can be together, and our problems are solved."

Magnus was eyeing the room, looking for an escape route. Nobody else seemed inclined to help him out of his predicament.

"Surely that would be cheating?" he asked.

"Well, if it is, what's another hundred years?" said Yoo Min. "I'd give it all up for you."

She leaned in towards him for a long sniff.

"I think that your liver would be very delicious."

Magnus coughed.

"...Thank you?" he said.

Yoo Min grinned up at him with her shark's smile.

"It's quiet in here," said Magnus. Quieter than it had been in some time, in fact.

He then noticed there were no ghosts around. They did not seem to make an appearance when Yoo Min was present.

Gears began to turn in his mind.

"Are you busy right now, Yoo Min?" he asked.

"Not really," said Yoo Min.

"Yes, you are," called Chief Ben from his desk.

Yoo Min glared at the stack of papers obscuring her boss from view.

"I'll have her back in half an hour, Chief," said Magnus.

"So I am supposed to trust a serial killer with my new officer?" Ben said.

"Don't worry!" Yoo Min sang. "I'll be fine."

She grabbed Magnus's hand and yanked him out the door. Magnus scrabbled at the handle to no avail as she pulled him down the hallway while Benandonner grumbled to himself about the possibilities of early retirement.

***

Yoo Min's idea of a romantic date was apparently the Necropolis, Glasgow's City of the Dead. The views were breathtaking, if the setting was morbid. She kept trying to take Magnus's hand, and he kept dropping it. She smiled anyway, as if that was what was supposed to happen.

"It's a beautiful day, isn't it?" said Yoo Min. "Look at the sky! The sun is out and it isn't very cold."

Magnus let her chatter, paying little attention. He was tired, and paranoid; but there was no sign of the ghosts, so he began to relax.

"...we could go on one of the ferries, down the Clyde!" Yoo Min was saying. "Wouldn't that be romantic?"

"*Stop!*" said Magnus loudly, startling himself. Yoo Min looked at him anxiously. He hung his head, curls flowing over his shoulder and hiding his face.

"You are unhappy with me?" asked Yoo Min.

Magnus shook his head.

"Then what is it, *oppa*?" she asked.

"*Stop calling me that,*" he said. "I know what it means. Stop."

Yoo Min looked across the view over Glasgow, and nodded.

"Yes," she said. "It means *older brother*. Yes, I see."

She knelt down in front of him and took his hands. She looked up into his eyes and was surprised to see him crying, tears falling to the earth at his feet.

"You feel guilt," she said. "You feel guilt, and we're monsters."

"Once, I took care of my brother," Magnus said. "I was the

responsible one. Dorian was a different man back then, and now…"

He couldn't speak further, as a sob rose in his throat demanding silence, and the tears threatened to consume him.

Yoo Min looked out over Glasgow and down at the Cathedral for a while before she spoke.

"Many years ago, my beautiful Magnus, I loved a man – a boy, he was. Just eighteen. He was one of the *Hwarang* – the servants of the queen – and he *loved me*. He would have denounced everything for me, and he believed there was more to me than the monster."

Yoo Min looked at Magnus's hands in her own, and tears also formed in her eyes. She looked up.

"There was not, Magnus," she said. "There was not more to me than the monster."

Magnus stared at her in horror.

"You…" he said, swallowing, his throat making an audible click.

Yoo Min nodded.

"I ate his liver," she said. "And he died without a single sound, and he still loved me. That was centuries ago. It was him – the reason I chose this path, why I became a police officer, and why I am here now. So you see, *oppa*, why I call you *older brother*, and why I am not disgusted – even though you are very large and your face is too big, and you would never be a *Hwarang*, I love you anyway."

Magnus sighed.

"Yes, Yoo Min, and I used to think I was in the right," he said. "Somehow I now feel that what I have done – it was very wrong."

Yoo Min smiled up at him.

"We can help each other," she said. "I can keep your ghosts away."

She gripped his hands.

"But you have missed something, *oppa*," she said, and stood.

She turned to look at him.

"What?" asked Magnus.

Yoo Min narrowed her eyes.

"This isn't about *you*, Magnus Grey," she said. "It never was. You are being very selfish."

Magnus was startled by the sudden change in her demeanour.

"This is about the humans," she said. "Your ghosts don't like this any more than you do. It's time we got involved in the investigation, and saved Leah Bishop."

Magnus shook his head and laughed.

"Leah Bishop doesn't need saving," he said. "Trust me, she's tough as nails."

Yoo Min looked at him like he was an idiot.

"No?" she asked. "She's at Gregoire's now, Magnus. She didn't come back to Glasgow. She's very sick."

Magnus's eyes widened. Leah had always seemed invincible. *Like us. Like one of the Fae.*

But she's human.

"I thought the worst thing that could happen to Leah was a bad hangover," he said.

His pocket started buzzing, and he reached into it to take out his phone.

"*Magnus Grey*," said a cold voice in his ear.

"Sebastian," said Magnus. Yoo Min was suddenly alert, her bright, foxy eyes watching him.

"I would not speak to you unless it were an emergency," snarled Sebastian. "But I want you to know that this has nothing to do with me."

"The hauntings?" Magnus said. "This isn't your revenge?"

"Hauntings?" asked Sebastian, surprised.

"Yes!" he said. "Your wife is here – well, she was – along with everyone else I –"

There was silence on the other end of the line. In the cavernous room where Sebastian stood, he put his hand on a silver frame set on a chest of drawers. The frame held a wedding photograph – happier days.

"Hazel?" he whispered.

"Yes," said Magnus. "Everyone! I can barely sleep."

"I will come to you," said Sebastian in a cold voice. "Now."
Click.

***

Sebastian stood in front of Magnus and Yoo Min in silence.

"Where –" he began.

"I'm here, Sebastian," said Hazel.

Sebastian turned. She was standing there, her eyes filled with tears, still beautiful. She held out her arms, and he rushed to her, only to grasp nothingness and a puff of smoke.

"Hazel!" he said, distraught.

"I'm here, my love," she said. "I'm here. You can't hold me, but I'm here."

And Sebastian, the greatest threat the supernatural world had ever known, knelt down and put his forehead to the ground in front of her. Silent tears fell. After a time, he looked up.

"How can you ever – the man I have become, Hazel..." he said.

She smiled.

"It doesn't matter," she said. "I'm here now. We can see each other again, and that was all I wanted. You can change, you know, Sebastian."

He stared at her, and the other people Magnus killed. They stood silent sentinel, watching.

His expression set, his mouth in a hard line.

"No, Hazel," he said. "I love you, but it's too late. You can stop haunting Magnus now. He has already been punished and awaits execution by faerie tribunal."

"So it really isn't you behind the hauntings?" asked Hazel, puzzled.

"No," he said. "I wouldn't have the faintest idea how. You were the witch, my love, not me. I know a few tricks, but mostly it's just psychology."

Everyone turned to look at Magnus.

"Don't look at me!" he said. "I wouldn't do this to myself."

"So Sebastian isn't behind the plague or the haunting," said Hazel, frowning.

"Why would I start a plague?" asked Sebastian. "I'm human too."

"No, you aren't, sweetheart," said Hazel.

Sebastian stared at his wife. His blood ran cold.

"Wh – what?" he asked.

"Sebastian, you look no different today than you did the last time I saw you," said Hazel. "You haven't aged at all. You're immortal, fae just like the rest of them."

Sebastian looked around as if to find some kind of denial in Magnus or Yoo Min's faces. Magnus seemed to take a particular joy in confirming what Hazel said.

"Yes," said Magnus. "Milo tested your DNA. You're supernatural, just like me."

He grinned in a way that was not altogether pleasant.

Sebastian's world was spinning. He couldn't think of anything to say.

"I – I'm not a *selkie*, am I?" Sebastian spat.

"No, thank God," said Magnus in horror. "Nobody knows what you are. You're something new."

Sebastian sat back on the ground, his head in his hands. Hazel looked at Magnus.

"It looks like we'll need to work together after all," said Hazel.

Sebastian looked up, disgust written across his features.

"What? You're not *working* with him, are you Hazel?!" he said. "He *murdered* you!"

"Yes, and believe me, he's paying for it!" said Hazel.

Magnus looked at Yoo Min, at Hazel, and finally Sebastian.

"Is redemption possible?" Magnus murmured, almost to himself.

Sebastian looked at him with all the deep-seated hatred he'd carried in his heart for decades.

"Not for you," he snarled.

He glanced up at his wife. His expression softened.

"And not for me, either. I am sorry, my love."

Sebastian stood up, a statue among the stones of the cemetery. He turned and walked away down the path, shaking his head as he went.

Hazel stared at his retreating figure with tears in her eyes.

"So he has become a monster," she said. "I had always hoped–"

Yoo Min looked up.

"You *knew*?" she asked.

Hazel nodded, biting her lip.

"I thought he could have a normal life," she said. "Normal enough, anyway."

Yoo Min stood and walked up to Hazel.

"And what were you going to say, when fifty years had passed, and you had aged, and he hadn't?" she demanded. "I know we are monsters, but you had no right!"

"I loved him, Yoo Min!" said Hazel. "And now I am shackled to the man who murdered me."

It was Magnus's turn to stand. He joined them, as the sun sank beneath the horizon of the city and the sodium lights began to spread an orange glow across the darkness of Glasgow.

"Hazel. I cannot take back what I have done," he said. "I wish I could. I wish I could take all of it back. But here we are – now. I am sure that Yoo Min's young man would also forgive her. He loved her, even though she hurt him."

"But I never loved *you*, Magnus Grey," said Hazel sharply. "You ask for forgiveness? I will never forgive the man who made a monster of Sebastian. My own death was not the end of me. There might be hope for Sebastian yet. But there isn't any for you."

Magnus stood, fists clenched, as darkness crept across the cemetery and the two women stared him down.

"Even if you will not forgive me, and even though I am a

monster, I will change," he said fiercely. "Even if I am executed by the faerie tribunal, I will be a different man when I step onto the gallows. And I will find out who is behind all this, which means we have to work together, Hazel."

Hazel pinned him with an imperious glare.

"But you will not take your brother down with you," said Hazel. "I won't see Dorian punished because of your selfishness. I will work with you for the sake of Leah Bishop and the other humans, but afterwards I never want to see your face again. Remember this, Magnus: you are nothing more than a monster to me."

Yoo Min laid a hand on his arm, and gave him a look full of meaning.

"And to me," she said. "Do not forget."

***

The streets and alleyways of Glasgow are cast orange beneath the soft light of sodium bulbs at night. The orange light of the city gives off a disarming warmth, as of a fireplace in a pub after a long night's traveling.

Those who live there know that warmth is an unlikely outcome of the evening, but the light offers a sense of home all the same.

The man walking down the alleyway, swinging a silver pocketwatch, was likewise something unexpected packaged into a delicate Victorian frame.

Dorian walked down the alley, the light glinting off the silver as he swung the watch back and forth.

There was a sound behind him. Dorian grinned to himself. Exactly as he expected, and right on schedule. He knew innately the kind of element his particular aesthetic tended to attract: those that felt he must be the kind of fool easily parted from his money.

They were wrong.

"Eh, pal, you lost?" said a voice.

Dorian half-turned. The smile on his face was unsettling. The man following him took a step back, suddenly uncertain.

"I've been waiting for you," Dorian said softly.

The man's cruel and vindictive laughter was a cover for his terror.

The suffering immediately thereafter, as Dorian let magic built over a century's disuse burst from his fingertips, was pure, silent, and without remorse.

Afterwards, Dorian stood, meticulously wiping the blood from his hands. His expression never changed.

Someone else was in the alley with him now; someone new. Someone whose hulking presence was difficult to miss, no matter how stealthy he thought he was being.

"How long have you been there?" Dorian asked, without turning around.

Benandonner stepped from the shadows.

"This is unacceptable, Dorian," said Chief Ben. "Those days are long gone."

Dorian stared at him, empty.

"So are the days of the Black Death, Ben," he said. "And I am fighting now the way I fought it then. If they want to fight dirty, I am all too willing to accept."

"What's gotten into you, Dorian?" asked the chief. "We don't even know who *they* are yet. If I didn't know any better, I'd say that was *emotion* in your voice."

Dorian stared at the man on the ground.

"The humans," said Dorian. "They are falling, Ben! You know the Fair Folk depend upon them, and always have. We are powerless to stop something that simply needs *antibiotics!* We are so *weak* against this! We are supposed to be the strongest creatures alive!"

Benandonner nodded.

"The humans," he said. "By which you mean Leah Bishop."

Dorian stared at him, and shut his mouth with a snap.

"Yes. It has been so long since I have had a friend. She is like a sister to me."

Ben regarded Dorian with a raised eyebrow.

"A sister, to replace the brother you already have?" asked Chief Ben.

"That *murderer* is not my brother," said Dorian.

"I rather think he is," said the chief. "You've nearly just murdered a human yourself, and you're a *police officer*, Dorian Grey!"

"He was not the kind of man who deserved to live," Dorian said. "Nevertheless, I spared his life."

"And who made you the judge, jury, and executioner? I've a mind to take you in for this myself!" said Ben. "We're *monsters*, Dorian, all of us. Including you. Magnus is frightened, and he may not be on Earth for much longer. He could use your support."

"I do not support murderers," sniffed Dorian.

"You don't have to agree with what he's done," said the chief, "but you could be there for him."

"I would rather *be there* for my partner," said Dorian. "But thank you for the advice."

Dorian turned away.

"There is a ransom," said the chief. "If we want the cure."

Dorian stopped.

"What do they want?" he asked.

"The key to *Tir Na n-Og*," Ben replied.

Dorian stared at him for a long time.

"And I assume you are telling me this for reasons other than the fact I am a detective?" he asked.

"Everyone knows the selkies guard the key to the Land of the Young," he said.

"No. Absolutely not," said Dorian. "There is no way."

"There's nobody left, Dorian," said Ben. "Milo can't find a cure. Doctors can't find a cure. We will lose Leah."

Dorian's resolve weakened.

"You cannot truly believe that this is a good idea," he said.

"Of course it's not a good idea!" said the chief. "But we're running out of time, and it's the only one left. Go back to Faerie and get the key."

CHAPTER ELEVEN

CESSNOCK BANKS

The once-clear water of Cessnock ran red with the blood of the Fae. Blood humans couldn't see, and raining down cannon that humans couldn't hear, the smoke filling the noses of any faerie-born that happened upon the site of the battle. Most kept well away, these days.

The one human who could see and hear it all was foolish enough to rush headlong into the battle, but then all humans are foolish, especially in love.

Robert sat with Desdemona and the other soldiers in the tent. He now wore the uniform, as he wanted to spend his remaining years fighting for the cause.

The transformation hadn't worked. Desdemona wasn't surprised, but Robert was heartbroken. All he wanted was to devote himself to her, under the guise of helping with the war effort, and he felt the opportunity had sifted through his fingers like falling sand.

He looked at her, strong and broad-shouldered with a soldier's bearing, close-cropped hair and skin filthy with the mud of the fields.

"Why is it that you look the way you do?" he asked her. "I thought *baobhan sith* were beautiful women with long red hair."

Desdemona, who had dozed off, cracked open one bright green eye.

"You saying I'm not beautiful, Robert?" she teased.

He blushed, stammering, and she took pity on him as her

expression became serious.

"It's because of the war," she relented. "I'd be too obvious out there, with red hair and pale skin. This way I blend in, and we can stay out of sight. What are you doing here, anyway?"

Robert opened the flap of the tent, and as the cool, fresh air circulated, he looked up at the stars.

"A faerie war?" he said. "Fighting side by side with a woman of supernatural origin? How could I not?"

"This is war, Robert," she reprimanded him. "Don't romanticise it."

He looked down, fiddling with his shirt cuffs. Desdemona gave him a long look.

"Creatures older than dreams are dying here tonight."

Robert was startled to see two men approaching the tent. He stood aside as they entered. Desdemona, in the midst of packing her pipe with tobacco, looked up and groaned softly under her breath. Robert shot her a quizzical look.

"Seal-men," she said. "Foppish, useless prettyboys. Mostly we have to save their skins. *Both* kinds."

"Magnus Grey," said the one with the curly hair, by way of introduction. "And my brother Dorian."

"And what can I do for you, men?" asked Desdemona, half-smiling. "You planning on being camp followers?"

"We would like to join in the fight," said Dorian.

"And get your hands dirty?" she laughed. "Well, I never thought I'd see the day."

"Please," said Magnus. "We are good fighters. Give us a chance."

"Fencing, maybe," said Desdemona. "And fencing with rules, at that. There's no fencing here, selkies. This is hard, bloody work, over in an instant. If you value your hides, you'll get the hell out of here."

Dorian stepped forward.

"Humans are dying," he said. "We must do what we can."

"Well, I won't say no to more cannon fodder," she said. "It's your funeral. Definitely."

Robert watched the two men leave the tent, and Desdemona shook her head.

"Selkies. Useless ornaments!" she muttered to herself. "What good can they possibly do? They're about to get themselves killed, or worse."

Iain, who had been cleaning his gun across from her and pointedly ignoring Robert Burns, finally looked up.

"I'm a selkie," he reminded her.

"Yes, thank you, Iain," she said.

She paced back and forth, shaking her head. Eventually, she stuck her knife into the table, walking out of the tent and muttering in disgust.

***

Iain pushed aside the flap of the tent and entered.

Desdemona was smoking, working on a map of the area and planning troop movement.

"Yes, Iain, what is it?" she asked, not looking up.

Iain's face wore an unfamiliar expression. Desdemona was startled to recognise it as sympathy.

"I'm sorry to report this," he said. "Robert Burns is dead."

Desdemona leaned back in her chair. She felt a stirring of emotion she could not categorise. Her green eyes were distant.

"On the battlefield?" she asked quietly.

Iain shook his head.

"No," he said. "He died of drink."

Desdemona sighed and shook her head.

"I knew it wouldn't work," she muttered to herself, just low enough that Iain wouldn't hear.

"A pity," she said out loud. "He was talented."

Iain, who knew her better than anyone, her best friend and comrade in arms, sat down in front of her. The softening of his usual strange and warlike gaze transformed his features, and it was clear why the seal-people had considered him their most beautiful.

He reached forward, as if to take her hand or to embrace her, but then seemed to reconsider.

"I'm sorry, Desdemona," he said, hesitant, the form of the words tasting foreign in his mouth.

Desdemona waved him off.

"Humans die, Iain," she said. "Go. You've got work to attend to."

Iain nodded, bowed, and left the tent.

Desdemona stared off into space, thinking. She wondered if she'd weep. It was an experience with which she was unfamiliar. She often wondered when it might happen the first time, but after thousands of years of travel, of experience and war, it was something she had yet to understand.

She waited. Nothing happened.

Then she shook herself, picked up her stylus, and went back to planning war.

St. Michael's Kirkyard
September 1815
Dumfries

The night was colder than expected, but one never knew what to expect in Scotland.

Interest in phrenology had caused a great deal of speculation about the national poet. Many people wished to know if he had anything in common with the greats of other nations and if anything could be learned from the shape of his skull.

The exhumation of Robert Burns was therefore undertaken in secret, so that his body could be moved to the larger, more impressive mausoleum at the other end of the cemetery without any interruption from the general public wanting to view the body.

The men worked silently, shoulder to shoulder. No one spoke. It didn't seem right.

"Here," said one of them, after the shovel hit something solid.

They dug around the coffin until the top was exposed.

Reverently, they went to push the lid off.

"Holy Christ," one of them swore softly.

Robert Burns looked merely asleep.

His entire body was intact, his features still handsome. It almost seemed as if he were breathing.

The men working on the grave were solid, serious Scottish gentlemen, chosen for their respect for Burns as well as their circumspection. They were not superstitious by any stretch of the imagination.

All of them were shaken. They stared in wonder at something they could not explain, their first experience with the supernatural.

In awe, one of them reached out a trembling hand and touched the poet's cheek.

Suddenly, Robert Burns' body fell to ash before their eyes, and only his bones remained.

The man who had touched his cheek cried out in horror. He lurched forward, driven by the automatic, mad desire to reshape the body. Distressed, the men dragged their compatriot away from the coffin. He was mumbling an apology, horrified at what he'd done.

"What are we going tae do now?" asked one of them. "How was it possible? He looked –"

"Alive," said the man who had touched his cheek, miserable.

"Weel, it's no' as if anyone else saw," whispered another man, "an' no one will ever know."

"The important thing is to keep those fools away from his body," said the first man, reassuringly, "sick bastards just wanting to measure his skull. No' going to tell them anything except that Burns had a skull."

"Haven't they heard of grave robbing?" muttered another in agreement.

They continued to comfort their friend as best they could, giving him some whisky to steady his nerves, and speaking together in quiet voices.

In the coffin, the ashes of the poet moved, and began to dance as if a soft wind were blowing, although it was a still night.

The ashes took form and shape, solidifying, recreating the strong, lithe body, and lastly, the handsome face with a slight blush to the cheeks that was the hallmark of the poet.

And on a cold September night in 1815, 19 years after his death, Robert Burns opened his eyes.

BATTLEFIELD, CESSNOCK BANKS

The lights were burning low, and Desdemona had nodded off, pistol in hand. A glass of whisky sat in front of her. The war seemed to go on forever, without pause or respite; Iain thrived in this environment, but Desdemona was ready for a cease fire. This war had lasted so long, she could no longer remember who she had been before it.

She became vaguely aware that someone had entered the tent. She lifted and pointed her gun without looking, still half asleep.

"Desdemona," said a voice she still heard in her dreams, sometimes. It was the voice that sparked thoughts of another life, a hope that something else might be in store for her beyond the endless blood and violence. A creature – for, to her, Robert Burns was a creature, just as she was to the rest of the world – who, for whatever his silly sentiments, was the last to see her as something other than a soldier.

She thought she was still dreaming. She did dream of him, at times, of a bright sun she'd never seen, and of a river flowing clean and quiet, because she heard a song of his once.

Not that she'd admit this to anyone.

She opened her eyes.

Standing there, covered in dirt, in a loose white shift with his black hair in his eyes, he somehow looked more handsome and luminous than ever he had as a living man.

"*Robert?!*" she said. "What the hell are you doing here?"

Robert shook his head, quite disoriented.

"They exhumed my body," he said. "I...someone touched me and that's all I remember."

Desdemona stood up and walked over to him, still with caution as she had learned from this endless war to trust nothing, not even her own eyes or senses.

"They're not going to like finding an empty coffin," she said, keeping her distance.

"It isn't empty," he said.

Desdemona stared at him.

"Don't ask," he said.

"But Robert...it's been *years*," she said.

"Yes," he replied. "I guess it worked."

Somewhat blindly, he reached out for her.

"Desdemona?" he said.

She backed away.

"What?"

"I'm *hungry.*"

CHAPTER TWELVE

SCOTTISH HIGHLANDS, PRESENT DAY

The atmosphere in Gregoire's cave had the feel of a cheery Highland afternoon. The fire crackled merrily and the urisk had just returned, stomping the snow off his boots and offering Leah the ubiquitous tea. He went to put on the kettle and busied himself at the pantry shelf she could just see from her vantage point on his sofa.

Dorian walked into Gregoire's cave. The kettle was merrily whistling on the stove as Leah turned over in bed and started up when she saw him. She grinned at her partner and sighed with relief.

"Oh, thank God," she whispered, "I didn't know how much tea I could drink before –

What is it? What's wrong?"

Dorian took a moment to speak. Leah looked much worse for wear and he wasn't sure how to proceed at first. He sat down on a stool, straight-backed, and was all business, mostly to cover his concern for the state of his partner.

"Whoever is responsible for the resurgence of the plague sent the chief a message at the police station," said Dorian. "They have the cure, but they want an exchange."

"What's the ransom?" Leah asked.

Dorian hesitated.

"They asked for the key to *Tir Na n-Og*." he finally said.

Leah, Robert, and Gregoire were all taken aback.

"The Land of the Young?" asked Leah. "Do you even have it?"

"Yes," said Dorian. "It is the responsibility of the selkies."

"Dorian, there is *no way* you are giving them the key to, well, Heaven!" said Leah.

"Leah. We cannot help you. I cannot help you," Dorian said. "Doctors are our only hope – magic can do much, but it cannot bring the dead to life and it cannot kill us either. We watch you age, we watch you get sick, we watch you die – but I have never felt this way about it."

"If you feel it's necessary, then I understand," said Leah.

"I think it is," sighed Dorian, tired to the marrow of his bones. "How are you, anyway?"

"I've been better, but it hasn't been a total loss," said Leah. "Robert has been visiting, telling me stories about the war."

Dorian froze.

"Oh dear," he said.

Leah smiled.

CESSNOCK BANKS

The soldiers were seated in Desdemona's tent, passing a flask to each other in the darkness. The enemy had moved closer and they could not afford to have any light give away their position.

"So, why'd you do it?" asked Magnus.

The other soldiers looked at him.

"Why'd you join?" he asked.

"For Dahlia," said Dorian, whose trim Victorian lines and close-cropped hair would become his new identity to the world. Dahlia was the woman who cried seven tears into the sea, and so Dorian was now one of the Taken selk. They would become what their betrothed wanted them to be, and frequently changed quite a bit from their native personality.

As for Aidan, it seemed like the young man was all but forgotten. Once a selkie answered the call, their former attachments faded into a sort of nothingness. Still, his eyes took on a faraway look whenever he heard mention of the ballet, or the dancers.

"I find that I have more of an interest in humankind, now that I am Taken," he said.

"I wanted to be a part of history," said Magnus.

"I have always been dedicated to the humans," said Gregoire.

"I wanted to prove to the Fae that the selkies aren't all useless, gentle creatures," said Iain vehemently, "that we, too, can be savage and merciless."

Everyone gave him a strange look. Desdemona raised an eyebrow and smiled at him.

They all looked at Desdemona last. She was smoking, and the embers of the pipe lit her features. She smiled and shook her head slowly.

"It was the right thing to do," she said.

Magnus and Dorian exchanged a glance.

"You're *baobhan sith*," said Dorian. "Since when do you have a moral code?"

Desdemona shot him a look.

"It's not exactly what I would call a *moral code*, selkie," she said. "Some things are just the right thing to do. Sometimes we choose them, regardless."

She studied the bowl of her pipe.

"I was addicted to the Smoke," she said. "Humans died because of me. People die because of me anyway – I'm a vampire. But this was heartless, soulless. This was evil. And evil is not a monster in the night, like us."

She leaned back and exhaled smoke at the ceiling.

"It's not the same," she said, indicating the smoke from her pipe, "but it'll do. There is no reason to waste human life on this scale. Eventually there will be no humans left, and then where will we be? We rely on them, for love or blood or both. It's just sensible."

Robert looked at her.

"What's it like?" he asked. "The Smoke?"

A lazy grin spread across Desdemona's face.

"Like nothing I've ever felt," she said. "Some vampires start human. We – the *baobhan sith* – never get a chance. The heart-beat, the wash of feeling, the taste of food. There is nothing like it."

She tapped her pipe.

"But it isn't real. It doesn't make you human, it's a faerie's fever dream. It drives you insane, eventually, because the Fae can't handle that kind of hallucination for an extended period of time. I dropped it after I saw others go mad with it. Getting off of the Smoke is a pain so excruciating you would prefer death, if death were a release the Fae could hope for."

"An altruistic vampire. I never thought I'd see the day," said Magnus.

Desdemona glanced up sharply.

"It's not altruism," she growled. "It's common sense, Magnus Grey. Humans are mortal. They die, we starve without dying. Selkies starved of love, your people wandering lonely. Gregoire's people never find the acceptance of the humans, or even the possibility of it. If you can name me one supernatural that doesn't need humanity I will be amazed. Humans need faerie stories. And we need them."

There was silence in the tent as they considered this. Desdemona stood.

"Right, men," she said. "Get some rest, if you're the kind of creature that needs it."

***

Robert grinned and stretched. Leah appreciated it. Dorian was blushing a strange colour Leah would never have expected to see in his pale cheeks.

Gregoire stoked the fire. Robert stood up.

"That's enough stories for one night," he said. "I need to get back to the hotel. Get some rest, Leah."

"Sure thing," she said. "Thanks, Robert."

"Of course," he said. "I'll be back tomorrow to check on you."

Robert left. Gregoire watched him go, warily.

"Wow, Dorian, you've had one hell of a life!" said Leah. "These stories are incredible! I wish you'd told them to me before, but I have to admit that having Robert Burns tell me bedtime stories is not something I'm going to complain about."

Gregoire looked into the fire.

"Well, there is one story Robert doesn't know. Isn't that right, Dorian?" he asked.

Dorian looked nervous.

"I don't think now is the best time," he began.

"Now is definitely the time, Gregoire. What do you mean?" asked Leah.

Gregoire glanced at Dorian, who stared at him, silently begging him not to speak.

Gregoire had other plans.

CESSNOCK BANKS

"Gregoire, can you move the most badly injured here to the front, please?" Desdemona called out.

The entire glade was filled with the groaning injured and the dying. Gregoire, the urisk medic, was tending to his patients as well as he could, given their limited supplies. He looked up at her and nodded. A few of his assistants set about making litters for the patients.

Desdemona knelt by one of her dying soldiers, her hand on his shoulder, whispering something. She rose to see Dorian and Magnus approach from the treeline.

"Hello," she said to the selkies. "If you want to make yourselves useful you can grab some of this ointment. We have other wounded to attend to; one of the Fae lost an arm but with Gregoire's stitching we'll get him back together again. It'll attach itself in no time."

She saw their stony expressions and her soldier's intuition

told her something was wrong.

"What?" she asked. "What is it?"

"Desdemona," said Magnus stiffly. "We are here on official business. Caledonia Interpol."

Desdemona barked a laugh.

"Those idiots?" she said. "Yes, well. What do they want now? There's a war on."

"You are under arrest for smuggling fae opium into Scotland."

Desdemona stared at them for a very long time.

"Interesting," she said evenly. "And exactly who informed Caledonia Interpol of that?"

Dorian looked at the ground. Magnus stepped forward.

"As of today, you are exiled," said Magnus. "Your offence is serious, but not serious enough to warrant execution. You have–"

Desdemona stepped into his space, ice and fury.

"Magnus Grey," she said, "I am the commander of the entire Fae battalion. If you remove me from duty I do not know what will happen. You must know that I would have nothing to do with the Smoke –"

"You are an *addict*," Magnus said in disgust.

"That was a long time ago," she replied. "I am not that person anymore. You cannot remove me from duty."

She put her face very near his, and spoke softly.

"I trusted you," she said, "and protected you on the battlefield when all the two of you could do was stir up some wind! I will not forget this betrayal."

"Magnus, maybe we should –" Dorian began.

"No, Dorian. Addicts are often liars," said Magnus, not taking his eyes off of Desdemona.

"So be it on your head, Magnus Grey," she said.

Magnus tied her wrists behind her. She stared at Dorian, who averted his eyes.

"Don't think you're innocent in this, Dorian," she said. "He's doing this out of sincere belief. You didn't defend me out of weakness. That's dishonourable, and unworthy of a warrior."

Magnus pushed her away from Dorian, toward the edge of the clearing.

"Good luck with the rest of the war," she told Dorian, as she passed by.

***

Robert walked through the forest, trying not to smile to himself like an idiot and failing spectacularly.

He'd gone on a few of his own adventures now as a vampire and noticed that he no longer marked time in the way he once did. It had been many years but he was eager to see the people he once fought side-by-side with, and he was fairly certain they would be where he had left them so long ago.

Robert was thrilled to be returning after all this time, to join his friends and Desdemona. Learning to be a vampire was not easy for him; it went against many aspects of his nature and his love for small living things.

He turned the corner in the wood, and it was empty.

Puzzled, he turned around himself. This was the clearing, he was certain of it. It had been several years since he'd been there, but he knew Desdemona hadn't moved camp in some time.

Had she left and not said goodbye?

"She's gone," said a voice. He turned to see Gregoire standing in the trees.

"Gregoire!" he said. "What's happened? Did you move camp?"

"No," he replied, "the camp is through here. Medical bay was too full, so we adjusted the location."

Robert began to follow and then stopped short.

"You just said she's gone," he said. "Gone? From here? From the war? From Scotland?" "Yes," Gregoire said.

"How?" he asked. "Why?"

Gregoire shrugged his shoulders, although he knew.

They entered the camp.

Robert's stomach revolted.

147

Blood and ichor was everywhere, the stench of the place was unbelievable. The cries of the wounded went to his heart and stayed there. As horrific as his first encounter with the medical area had been, it was nothing compared to the suffering spread out before him.

"What's happened, Gregoire?" he whispered.

"Without her," Gregoire said faintly, "this is how the tides of war have turned."

***

In Paris, the moon shone on cobblestone streets.

Desdemona was *baobhan sith*.

She'd been foolish to sacrifice the strength and tradition of life as a vampire in order to help the Fae and the humans.

Her hair was long and red again, her smile razor sharp, her eyes blazing green embers into the night.

Her clothes were green, and the robe fell away from her body, shimmering, as she stepped on the stage. The music began to play, and she swirled the veil around herself.

Forget.
This is who you were meant to be.
War, and fighting, and Robert Burns –
Forget.
Ridiculous human nonsense.
Be beautiful. Dance. Feed.
That is all you are worth, after all.

CESSNOCK BANKS

The battlefield at Cessnock Water was silent.

Birds had returned to the forest, and made sleepy coos from the trees.

Iain sat morosely with his gun by his side, forgotten. He loved that thing and polished it like it was his prize possession. Now, he just sat, staring off into the distance.

Robert approached and sat down beside him.

"Hello, Iain," he said. Iain's eyes flicked toward him and then down.

"You miss her too?" he asked. No response but a quick tightening of the seal-man's lips.

Robert looked out over the forest, the cots of the wounded.

"Well, I miss her," he sighed. "I always do. Now it's worse."

He put his arms on his knees, his hands hanging down. He sighed, and closed his eyes.

Gregoire stepped out of the last remaining tent. He would be the last to leave, as he was looking after the sick and dying. He looked up at a sky, the gloaming filling the place with purple and lavender darkness.

There was only a split second of silence.

Then there was a pinprick of light in the sky.

And Gregoire knew, as the light fell and expanded, that once again he would have to collect the scraps in the aftermath. He shielded his head with his arms and braced himself, wondering how they were able to get such an accurate bead on their location. He didn't even have time to call out a warning to the others.

Without Desdemona, there was no respite, and no hope.

The explosion shook the earth, down deep where the creatures that had no interest in the ongoing war for humankind lived.

The light was brilliant, and consumed them all.

***

In Paris, the moon shone on.

***

Rain fell softly on the cobblestones, the murmur of the water turning the street silver-white. Two figures stood waiting in front of a door that suddenly opened, suffusing them in a warm and intoxicating glow of incense and candlelight.

The room was a dark and gaudy fantasy of Arabia, rich hangings and cushions, smoke curling from pipes. Young men lounged in various attitudes around the room.

The woman at the centre was more stark than beautiful. Her white skin stood out against the cushions; her fiery hair curled over a bare shoulder. She put a cigarette to lips as red as the velvet, with delicate fingers ending in long nails keen as razor-blades. Colours around her brightened in comparison.

Life is livelier around death.

The door opened, and a breath of night air moved through.

"Messieurs Dorian et Magnus Grey," announced the man at the entrance. The men in the chamber turned towards the door, vaguely curious in their opium haze.

Desdemona sat up as she recognised the newcomers, shaking the rain from their cloaks.

"Seals," she said, "What are you doing so far from the sea?"

"We could ask you what you are doing here," said Magnus, his voice gentle, soft, insinuating, as he looked around the room. The young men struggled to their feet, despite their state of delirium, and crowded around her in defence.

"It's all right," she said to them, smiling with white teeth, "these are...old...*friends*."

The young men resumed their original positions, but all had turned toward the selkies, watching them with wary eyes.

"Desdemona –" Dorian began.

"*You had me banished, Dorian Grey*," she snarled, "You know *exactly* what I am doing here. Your kind is not welcome."

"You'd prefer life in the Highlands? Everyone *died*, Desdemona! *Everyone.* The Highlands are empty. You don't want to be there."

"You had no right to make that choice for me," she said. "*They were my people too.*"

"You fed on them," said Dorian, "Your kind were making

things worse."

"I'm a *vampire*, Dorian!" she said, "It's what I *do*. Humans eat steak. Selkies eat fish. You're a hypocrite. You can't banish an entire Highland species! *They are my people too.*"

"You're set up well here," said Magnus, looking around the chamber, and at the plentiful supply of both food and wine, "You're in Paris, in the centre of art and culture, with men on whom you are able to feed. I don't see what you have to complain about."

"When you are exiled, you can tell me how it feels," said Desdemona, "Come with me. I'll show you something."

She stood and walked into the back of the room, and pulled on a golden rope. A red curtain moved aside to reveal a staircase winding away into darkness. They followed her down the steps into the underground chill. At the bottom, the staircase opened out into a cavernous wine cellar. Countless bottles lined the walls, and stood lone sentinels on barrels, covered with dust. Her white hand touched one of them, and she pulled out a bottle from the rack, handing it to Dorian.

She looked at him, her green eyes bright.

"I have travelled the entire world, Dorian Grey," she said, "I hadn't returned to Scotland in centuries. Word came to me of the suffering there, and so I returned in secret. Although it had changed much and seemed strange to me, the land – the bones of the country – remained the same. I knew it as I know myself."

She paused, remembering. She indicated the bottle Dorian held in his hands.

"Here," she said, "is blood from a woman in 1746, just after Culloden. I taught myself how to bottle it. Like wine, it improves with age."

"You *were* part of the suffering!" said Dorian, "how could you do this at the worst possible -"

"Dorian," Desdemona interrupted gently, "let me explain. This woman gave me her blood in exchange for safe passage out of the country for herself and her children. A vampire, by night, can do many things – and inspire fear – when others cannot. Especially a *baobhan sith* who knows the dark and lonely roads of the Highlands. The loss and suffering was too much for us to bear, and many of us – including me! – changed our ways to prevent the further sorrow of our people. Then, as now, I drink only enough to stay alive. I drink what is *freely given*. This woman lived a long and full life! So do her children, who today prosper because we monsters chose to do what others would not."

Desdemona gestured at the bottles.

"*All of this* comes from people I helped," she said, "escape to America, to France, to anywhere Scotland was welcome. There are Scots all over the world because *I helped them*. Think of how they may have been annihilated if they had not been able to emigrate! Scotland's children survive, the various bloodlines intact, *because vampires helped them cross the sea*. So get off your high horse, selkie, you have limited imagination."

Dorian stared around the room. He touched one of the bottles.

"And this?" he asked.

"That's the champagne rack," said Desdemona, "I like to drink the blood with alcohol, since this commitment means that many *baobhan sith* are in a state of permanent near-starvation. Absinthe is best, and seems as though it were made for the purpose. The alcohol doesn't do much for me, but I enjoy the flavour."

She sighed, folding her arms across her chest.

"I'm a vampire, in the end," she said, "There is no real way I can be considered on the side of good. I saw what happened to our people, the starvation and the suffering. I watched the soldiers...Scottish soldiers, on King William's side. It seemed, in fact, that King William's side was the Scottish side, as there were more Scots with him than with Charles. The soldiers refused to help any of their own, even women who were not allowed to drink the blood of their own slaughtered cattle. They starved to death. Starved, while the soldiers watched and laughed."

She looked down, tears in her eyes.

"*I saw our people die too, Dorian.* So I helped in the only way I knew how. Even monsters have their limit, and that was mine."

"I am sorry, Desdemona," said Dorian, "I had no idea."

"Of course you didn't," she said, rounding on him, "that's who you both are – strike first, ask questions later. Your recruitment to the police force is not a surprise."

"I like to think I am not like my brother," offered Magnus.

"I know you do," Desdemona replied, "and you're wrong."

She shook her head, and turned away. She climbed the stairs again, returning to the warmth of the room above. The selkies followed her, and as she returned to her seat the doorman announced another name.

"If you'll excuse me, boys," she said, "I have some friends coming to visit, and you must go. Give my love to Scotland. I will return one day, despite the edicts. It is my home, whether you like it or not."

A handsome young man had entered, and he bowed to them as they were ushered by the doorman out into the night. The room with its rich tapestries and pillows vanished like a fevered dream as the door shut, leaving the two men alone on a front step that gave no indication of the world behind the front door.

Outside, the fresh and damp air of a spring evening seemed too real, as Dorian and Magnus breathed in the cool night and exhaled steam. As if the door had closed on another world, Paris by comparison seemed to hold no magic. The sky was dark, and rain fell as the selkies pulled their cloaks close around their shoulders.

"Well, that shows us," shrugged Magnus.

Dorian said nothing, but kept his head down as they walked, and spoke not a word the rest of the evening.

CHAPTER THIRTEEN

GREGOIRE'S CAVE

The silence in Gregoire's cave made the crackling of the fire sound even louder.

Leah stared at the urisk and her partner in turn.

"Did she do it, Dorian?" Leah murmured. "Did she smuggle opium during the war?"

Dorian looked at the floor, wretched.

"No," he said flatly. "We were wrong."

"So that's why she hates you," said Leah. "Did Robert ever find out what happened to Desdemona?"

"No," said Gregoire. "But he assumed the worst. Eventually, he gave up looking. As far as I know, he never stopped loving her. I sometimes wonder if he'd have been a different man. I wonder many things.

"He had a good life, for all that."

The intensity of Leah's air of consternation would not have allowed her eyebrows to stay on her forehead with the way she was raising them.

"What the *hell*, Dorian? You have to tell him!" said Leah.

Dorian shrugged.

"She never loved him," he said. "It's for the best."

"Will you ever get it through your head that it's *not up to you*?" asked Leah. "Maybe it doesn't matter! Have you ever told him that it was your fault? And Magnus's? You betrayed her, and you were wrong. Then you hide it from Robert all these years! Dorian, I thought he was your friend!"

"Yes, he is! And there is not a night that has gone by since that I do not chastise myself for it!" Dorian snapped. "But it is a wound that will never heal. This love – there's something fey in it. There's something strange in that kind of myopic, intense focus on one being."

"Says the selkie," Leah shot back.

"In anyone who *isn't* a selkie," he clarified. "She'll never love him back. She can't. She's incapable of it. He couldn't survive it. Not this long."

"But he *has*," Leah insisted. "The only other thing he talked about, or told stories about, besides you – was her! He still loves her just as he did then."

"The romance of nostalgia," Dorian said.

"I don't think so," said Leah. "You yourself said there's something fey in it. Let someone have what neither of us did, Dorian. Give her back to him."

"She's not mine to give," sniffed Dorian.

"Don't you dare switch things around like that and make it sound like it's a feminist choice," said Leah. "You screwed this up. Make it right. Maybe he'll hate you, but at least he'll know. Then he can choose for himself."

Dorian adjusted his cufflinks and wouldn't look at her. He stood up.

"Right now, what is important is making you well. I must leave now. We are running out of time."

Leah stood, swaying a little, arms crossed, in Gregoire's mad tartan fantasy cave.

"This is *ridiculous*, Dorian!" she said. "I am your *partner*."

"And you are human, and it isn't safe," he said.

"What happened to *you have weapons, Leah Bishop*?" she shot back at him.

"Remember when I told you there would be times that I would need to help you, just as you helped me?" he asked. "This is one of those times."

Dorian turned to go, and Leah started to walk towards him.

The selkie turned around and she was startled to see an anger there flare up, his eyes went bright blue and then extinguished.

"*Stay here, Leah!*" he shouted. "I will not ask again!"

"You try using your powers on me, I am *so* going to kick your arse from here to next Tuesday," Leah snapped back.

Dorian turned smartly on his heel and walked out of the cave. Leah huffed in annoyance. She went back to the sofa, feeling a little dizzy with the effort of standing. She felt a warmth at her elbow, and saw Gregoire's ugly features written with concern as he set down a cup of tea beside her.

"Do not feel too angry with Dorian. I don't often see that expression on his face," said Gregoire.

"What's that? Superiority?" asked Leah. "'Cause I can tell you, he wears it all the time."

"No, Leah. Fear."

Leah lifted her eyes to the monster's.

"I have never seen him so terrified. Not since before, during the worst of the fighting," said Gregoire. "He thinks this will be the end."

***

On a beach, in the darkness as the sea washed against the shore, lonely and cold, a seal pulled itself onto land. There was a strange, liquid sound of tearing, and a hand emerged as the eyes went dull. The skin was pulled apart, and Dorian slid out, holding a silver key in his hand.

***

"What are we doing here, Magnus?" asked Hazel.

Magnus stood outside a bar he'd frequented when he was a free man. He paused in front of the door.

"Trying to drink all of you away," he said, glancing around at the number of shades still pursuing him.

"This is a terrible idea," she said. "I don't think you should."

"Doesn't matter what you think," he said. "I'm free of your hold on me now, and you're not in charge here,"

"I'll tell Chief Ben," she warned. Magnus shrugged.

"Then I'll pay for it later," he replied. "They've already got me in the Deeps. What's the worst he can do?"

"I'll tell Dorian," she said. He stopped at this, clearly indecisive. Then he shook it off.

"You don't have a mobile phone," said Magnus. "Anyway, he's obviously chosen a side. So what're a few drinks going to hurt?"

Magus pushed through the door into the pub, where he took a seat at the bar. He winked at the woman sitting next to him. Hazel rolled her eyes. She was surprised that he was up to his old tricks, but she also felt she should've known. The woman beside him made a disgusted noise in her throat and turned away. Magnus did not seem deterred. Even in the circumstances, the selkie didn't seem to realise his advances were unwanted.

Magnus turned on his bar stool and immediately began smiling at the other woman sitting next to him. She looked him over, took in his beautiful features and long hair, and smiled back.

"Can I buy you a drink?" he asked.

"Sure," she replied.

His murder victims flickered into existence all around him. There was a chill in the air that moved through the bar.

No one else could see the women and men surrounding Magnus with blood on their faces. The creep show was for him and him alone, but he seemed to have gotten used to it. The selkie leaned over and started to speak to the woman, ignoring the ghosts crowding in close around him.

Hazel leaned over and screamed into his ear at the top of her lungs.

Magnus leapt up as if he had been stung, knocking over his barstool in the process. The woman seated next to him gave him a strange look.

"Are you all right?" she asked. Magnus righted his barstool, looking hunted.

One of the bloodied ghosts leaned in towards him.

❦ CHAPTER THIRTEEN ❦

"Well, Magnus," said Kathryn, grinning through bloodied teeth, "it looks like you might be off your game."

Naomi, another ghost, took a handful of his curly hair and yanked as hard as she could. He went over again, flailing, onto the ground. The woman who had been seated beside him stood up.

"Whatever you're up to, I don't want to be a part of it," she spat, and left in a hurry. Not without taking her free drink, though.

"Wait..." Magnus called after her, to no avail. He sighed. Hazel smirked. She took out a cigarette from God knows where and put it into a fine black holder, lighting it and breathing out smoke.

"How did you –" he began, before doing some mental arithmetic and turning to Naomi instead.

"So, Naomi," he leered, "If all of you can interact with the physical world, there's a lot of opportunity there, if you get my drift. If you can do that, imagine what we all could do together."

"We're ghosts, Magnus," said Hazel. "The selkie charm doesn't work anymore. On any of us."

Magnus looked defeated. Hazel smiled.

"There is *one* thing," she relented.

Magnus looked hopeful again.

"Bartender," called Hazel. The bartender approached her.

"Wait. He can see you, but that woman couldn't?" asked Magnus.

"Freedom of choice, Magnus," said Hazel. "We're seen when we want to be seen."

The bartender looked closely at her, and her cigarette.

"No smoking indoors, miss," he said. "I'm sorry."

"Quite all right," said Hazel, and the cigarette vanished.

"Neat trick," said the bartender.

"Thank you," she replied. "Now, could I order a round of drinks for my friends here? He's buying."

She tipped a wink at Magnus, who suddenly realised he'd gotten himself into a situation here.

"Coming right up," said the bartender, who paused for a moment. "Er…you and your friends look a little – I mean, shouldn't you be going to hospital?"

Hazel laughed, a bright sound. Magnus was stunned, but also somewhat impressed by her bravado.

"Oh, no," she said. "Zombie walk."

The bartender blushed, embarrassed.

"Oh yeah," he said. "Of course, I knew that. So what can I get you?"

The ghosts put in their orders. Magnus produced his wallet, knowing they could affect him physically and were not above pretty much any kind of retaliation. What money he had left slowly drained away before his eyes.

The ghosts of his victims sat around Magnus, occasionally shoving him or poking at him as they laughed together, talking about old times. The bartender arrived with their glasses, filled with all kinds of strange concoctions. They'd made a point of ordering the most complicated, expensive cocktails on the menu. As the drinks were passed around, Magnus sighed and seemed to curl inwards on himself. He was certainly getting the night out on the town he wanted, if not in the way he'd have wanted it.

"Right, everyone," Hazel announced. "Let's drink!"

Magnus sat in the centre of the horseshoe-shaped booth looking miserable, as the ghosts all drank their cocktails. The ghosts flickered in and out of sight depending on who was passing by, and they laughed uproariously every time a woman gave him a strange look, only seeing a pathetic young man drinking alone.

***

Milo sighed and set down his tools. He looked up at Dorian.

"That was my last idea," said Milo. "I'm sorry. There is really no cure."

"That can't be right," said Dorian.

"Sometimes you have to let go," Milo replied.

Hazel was staring curiously at Yoo Min, who eventually noticed.

"Yoo Min, are you feeling all right?" she asked.

"Yes, why?" asked Yoo Min.

"Well she can't be sick, she's not human," said Magnus.

"I didn't ask you, Magnus," Hazel said. "But that's not what I mean. Are you hungry?"

Yoo Min laughed.

"Well, yes," she said. "That's what a hundred years of starvation will do."

"What?" asked Hazel, concern etched into her voice. "Why are you starving yourself?"

"Because the legend goes that after 100 years of denying herself liver, a gumiho can be cured. The suffering is difficult, but I made a promise to someone," said Yoo Min, touching the pendant on her necklace.

"Oh," said Hazel, "But it's not true, Yoo Min. It's a lie they spread to kill off your kind."

"Are you serious?" asked Dorian. "Hazel? How do you know?"

"I'm a witch," she said. "I can see her lifeline and she is nearly at the end. You know how only certain things can kill the Fae? This is one of them. You're dying, Yoo Min."

Yoo Min stared at her.

"But I've starved for so many years," she said, uncertain.

"I know," said Hazel. "But it's not healing you. You need to eat."

"I can't! I won't kill again," said Yoo Min.

"What do you mean?" said Dorian. "You're always asking Magnus."

"I'm hungry!" said Yoo Min. "It's difficult. But I am so close!"

"You are not," said Hazel. "You will die. Soon. If you don't eat."

"I refuse to take another life. I promised Tae Pyeong," said Yoo Min.

"Then take a liver from someone who will not die," said Hazel, with a significant look towards Magnus.

Everyone present looked at the selkie. Magnus was horrified.

"I will contact the king," said Dorian, deep in thought. "This may be a suitable punishment."

"Dorian, you want to recommend that I let a monster *eat my liver*?" Magnus asked.

Milo grinned at this, and the ghosts all looked quite pleased.

"How often do you need to feed, Yoo Min?" asked Dorian, ignoring his brother.

"Once weekly, at least, but generally every day," said Yoo Min.

"Dorian, *no*," said Magnus.

"Wait here," said Dorian, taking his mobile phone out of his pocket.

Yoo Min gave Magnus a loving look, and smiled wide.

***

Gregoire noticed that Leah was awake again, and restless.

"You're very ill, Leah, you need to rest," he said.

"I'm going crazy, Gregoire," she said. "I need to do something to help. Research, or – wait, do you have wifi?"

Gregoire smiled proudly.

"I have all the modern human conveniences," he said.

Leah opened her laptop.

***

In the court of the selkies, the Seal-King took his throne.

"Dorian Grey proposes that the gumiho is offered Magnus's liver," he announced. "She will be allowed to consume it every day, to keep the human population safe from her hunger. This Promethean scenario will teach him guilt and humility under her knife.

"If you find this an appropriate punishment, say aye."

The room filled with a chorus of *ayes*. The Seal-King nodded.

"Let the record show that the education of Magnus Grey begins tonight. I only hope his suffering will teach him the error of his ways."

***

Dorian stood in the darkness of a closed restaurant, the key in his hand.

A tall, broad man entered and walked up to him.

"You're clearly not who I want to be speaking to," Dorian said.

"I'm here on his behalf," said Lachlan, and Dorian noted the word *his,* which he had not known before. "Did you bring it?"

Dorian held up his hand and let the key fall, suspended in the air on a string.

"First, the cure," he said.

"The key," demanded Lachlan, who brandished a truncheon.

"I can sense from here that you are human," said Dorian. "I really think attacking me would be unwise."

"Fine. He says the cure is healing fire. Now, the key."

Dorian was puzzled.

"Care to elaborate?" he asked.

Lachlan shrugged.

"That's all he said. Healing fire. Said you'd know what that meant."

"The key to *Tir Na n-Og,*" said Dorian, lifting his hand. A skeleton key shone in the low light. "I would tell you to use it wisely but I feel the advice is wasted."

Lachlan snatched the key out of his hand. Dorian nodded and turned away.

The man raised his truncheon.

"Do you think I would just let you walk out of here?" he demanded.

Dorian sighed.

"If you're going to make a joke about seal clubbing," he said, "at least have the decency to knock me out first so I don't have to hear it."

163

Suddenly, Lachlan collapsed in front of him. Dorian looked up in shock to see Sebastian standing there.

"What...?" he said.

Sebastian tossed him the key, and Dorian caught it.

"Get out of here," he said. "You don't have much time."

"Why would you help me?" asked Dorian.

"Don't imagine I did this for you, selkie," he said.

Sebastian turned and began to walk away.

"Then why?" asked Dorian.

Sebastian stopped. He turned his head to the side, as if to look over his shoulder. His eyes flickered downward, and the word *Hazel* remained unspoken, but understood.

***

Yoo Min stood in front of Magnus, who disrobed in front of her.

She laid him down on the floor, his hair spread around his head like a halo. She gazed at him with an expression of near-love and absolute hunger. She slowly took out her blade and carved into him as he screamed and screamed. She continued to stare at him in adoration, her expression unchanging in response to his suffering.

She was professional. Exact.

She began to eat the pieces of his liver, her hands bloody, tears spilling from her eyes as the blood pooled around him. His body began to heal, slowly, and eventually he lay there with unbroken skin, sticky with his own blood.

The ghosts in attendance faded away. The sacrifice was sufficient.

Yoo Min wiped her mouth and sighed, sated.

"Thank you, Magnus," she said.

Magnus stretched a hand out to her weakly, exhausted.

"You love me," he said. "It was a sacrifice."

Yoo Min regarded at him, uncomprehending, as if he had said something that confused her. Then understanding dawned on her face, and she looked at him with pity.

"I love Tae Pyeong," she said. "I never loved you, Magnus. I only wanted your liver."

Magnus stared at her with growing horror, a selkie fooled by the same manipulation he once used against others. She smiled sweetly.

"And you will give it to me every day," she said. "Your people have decreed it.

In this way, you will learn real sacrifice – and atonement."

She stood up to leave.

"But don't worry, *oppa*. I was right," she said. "You are *delicious*."

CHAPTER FOURTEEN

The cell door clanged shut as Magnus was once again locked inside. Dorian and Yoo Min stood beside Milo and Ben as they made sure the lock held fast.

"Well, the ghosts surrounding Magnus have all disappeared," said Chief Ben. "It must have been something about his sacrifice."

"Not *all*," said a voice.

They turned to see Hazel still sitting there.

"Hazel? Why haven't you faded?" asked Milo, surprised.

"I don't know," Hazel replied.

"I do," Yoo Min replied.

They looked at her curiously.

"Hazel is still here because she loves Sebastian," said Yoo Min. "And whatever kind of monster he is, and whatever he claims, he's bound her here. Or rather, he's cut her free."

"Yes, I think you're right. I can sense it; I am not bound to Magnus anymore," said Hazel.

"You're not bound to anyone," said Yoo Min. "Call it Sebastian's gift to you. He doesn't think he can change, but he doesn't want you to suffer. His magic was strong enough to do this for you, at least."

"So...why don't I vanish, then?" asked Hazel.

"I think you have the potential to," said Yoo Min. "But he left it up to you, because he felt it was a choice you did not have when Magnus killed you."

Everyone stared at Yoo Min, stunned.

"What?" she asked. "I don't think very well when I'm hungry. I do much better on a full stomach."

Dorian tried very hard not to remember the reason she now

had a full stomach.

"They made me a detective too, remember?" said Yoo Min.

Chief Ben turned to Hazel.

"Well, we could use someone who can walk through walls," he said. "If you've been bored beyond the veil, I think we could offer you a job here if you want one."

***

Leah sat in front of her laptop, holding her tea. She was still not feeling well but was content, although she was impatient for Dorian to return. She started her research on the urisk and began to read.

Humans fear the urisk...these creatures do not interact with humanity at all, despite their natural kindness...

Leah looked around Gregoire's cave, at the tartan blankets, the postcards of Scottie dogs and mountains and Shetland ponies, the tea cosy.

"How did he get all these things?" Leah mused to herself. "I don't think Ikea delivers to waterfalls."

Not like it was in the days of the runners...like Prohibition... and...

wifi...

wifi?!

Leah slowly looked up from her laptop at Gregoire, who was busily washing dishes in the kitchen, singing a *puirt á beul* to himself.

...it was common, like cocaine in jars next to the sugar...

Leah looked at the counter where the loose-leaf tea was kept in jars. She looked down into the mug she was drinking from, and then watched as her blackened fingers bruised a touch more; not enough to tell, if she hadn't been looking, but enough to convince her.

ohshitohshitohshitohshit

Leah's inner monologue drummed quietly at her, as she realised she would have to make sure Gregoire hadn't noticed a difference.

Gregoire had noticed her looking.

"Do you want some more tea, Leah?" he asked. "I'll just put the kettle on."

Leah smiled and nodded nervously. She couldn't quite believe it. He seemed so kind. Nurturing.

Gregoire handed her the tea. She stared at him, and then sipped the tea, her hands shaking.

"Are you not feeling well, Miss Bishop?" asked Gregoire, his formality reminding her strongly of her partner. She wished Dorian would hurry up and return to the Highlands; she couldn't do much in her current state.

"Dorian never has his phone with him," she thought to herself. "Who can I text?"

She saw in her mind's eye, Yoo Min always on her phone. Always.

She went online and sent a message, briefly detailing the situation, saying

they were wrong about how the Black Death spreads, just like the humans were...come as soon as you can.

It's in the tea. All of it. It's not in the air or the water. It's the tea.

She felt a wave of the illness taking over, and she fought against it, but it consumed her. She fell unconscious, and Gregoire caught the mug before it could fall to the floor.

***

Later that day, Dorian entered the cave with Nour-el-ain.

"We came as soon as we could," said Dorian.

"Thank you for coming," said Gregoire, "but I think it is too late."

Nour-el-ain and Dorian both looked down at Leah's still form. Gregoire held one of Leah's blackened hands in one of his large, blue-grey ones.

"It's all right, Gregoire, we found the cure," said Dorian. "The man that we were to trade the key said that healing fire was the only thing that would cure her. Are you ready, Nour-el-ain?"

"Yes," she replied.

She put her hands to the kettle and blue fire leapt from her fingertips as she heated the water inside. They poured it out into a mug and brought it to Leah, who was barely conscious. Nour wrapped Leah's fingers around the handle.

"Leah?" said Nour. "Drink this. Wake up, Dorian's here. He's very worried."

"Dorian?" said Leah, in a sleepy voice. "Dorian can't be here, it's dangerous."

Nour was instantly alert.

"Dangerous?" she asked. "Why?"

"Gregoire..." croaked Leah.

Nour looked sharply at the urisk just as he was about to attack her. Blue flame burst from her fingertips, covering both Leah and the phoenix. Dorian was horrified as Nour barely held Gregoire back with her healing fire.

"*Gregoire?!*" Dorian cried, betrayed. "It was you?!"

"Yes," growled Gregoire.

"But...why?" asked Dorian.

"Why?!" Gregoire spat. "You don't know?"

"The Smoke kills *everyone*, Fae and human alike!" said Dorian.

"That is **exactly** why, Dorian Grey!!" said Gregoire.

"I don't understand," said Dorian.

"Have you ever?" Gregoire snarled. "All the death? The suffering? Humans, faeries, the blood and bone, it all blends together in the end. Everyone just...wants to cause so much *suffering!*"

"I was in the war, too!" said Dorian.

"*Were you?*" Gregoire demanded. "Did you spend *centuries* tending to the wounded in a war that seemed like it would stretch on, twisting around itself, forever in both the future and the past? See the creative torture that humans caused – and since they have had more time, the tortures the Fae thought up for each other?"

"That is no excuse to cause more of it!" said Nour-el-ain.

"They never died," said Gregoire in anguish. "They *never died* and they had to go on and on, suffering! Like Desdemona told us, we live for them, they live for us, and the only way to end the suffering is to break the cycle."

"I trusted you with Leah," said Dorian bitterly. Gregoire ignored him.

"The war must end," he said. "The war must end. I am so tired. I still hear the explosions. I still see the dead.

"One day, I saw a man who had been cut in half. The top of the wall had been razor sharp, and they had sat him upon it as though he would sit astride a horse...and they **pulled.** He was split in half and he was Fae, so he was not dead, he felt everything. Everything! It took me days to find the other half of his body, on the other side of the wall, and both halves were still screaming. I stitched him together, in the end, but he was never the same.

"The Smoke heals as it kills. The humans, the beloved humans, will be free.

"How can you not understand, Dorian? You have loved them, too.

"Centuries of rejection. I have collected every piece here lovingly only to be spurned. I have grown to hate our kind, to hate my face as they have.

"Mutual destruction is the only answer."

"The war is *over,* Gregoire!" Dorian said.

"It's never over!" shouted Gregoire.

"The Nuckelavee died!" Nour interjected. "Glasgow was left vulnerable."

"Does it matter?" asked Gregoire. "In the end, the humans will not need protecting. The lesser evil, for the greater good."

"Humans are dying!" said Dorian. "By the thousands!"

"Then let them die!" snarled Gregoire.

"Why did you want it?" asked Dorian. "Why did you want the key to *Tir Na n-Og*?"

"Isn't it obvious, Dorian?" asked Gregoire. "The evil must be cut off at the head. The Smoke would kill them all, and destroy *Tir Na n-Og* forever. The humans would be free, and we would too.

"Leah Bishop will be the first sacrifice. I am sorry; I liked her. She was the first human who talked to me."

"That is not going to happen," said Dorian.

"And who will stop me? You?" demanded Gregoire.

"No," replied Dorian. "She will."

Yoo Min stepped forward out of the shadows.

"You would do this, for a human you just met?" asked Gregoire.

Yoo Min smiled.

"No. I will do this because I am the only monster left."

She moved swiftly, with her blade, everything quick and clean. She was not a fighter. She was a shark. And with her hands and mouth spread with blood, her eyes flickered.

"*I'm* the crazy one," she added.

She nodded to the others.

"Let's go home."

***

Everyone at Caledonia Interpol was having takeaway. The scent of chicken tikka masala filled the office, as much as it could; a light snow was falling. In the office. The tikka masala was a mysteriously bright orange colour, but that was to be expected.

Leah pushed Dorian's chair with her foot so he rolled away.

"Robert *Burns*, Dorian, what the hell," she grinned at him, between bites.

"I really couldn't resist," Dorian beamed. "I'm glad you're better."

Leah grinned back.

"I'm glad I get to be here for your annual smile," she said. "You should make it a national holiday."

"You can thank whatever gods you follow that Leah Bishop

studies folklore," said Milo. "Otherwise we'd never have suspected Gregoire."

The door opened, and Robert walked in. Dorian's expression grew serious.

"Hi everyone," he said. "Dorian, why did you want me to come all the way down to Glasgow?"

Dorian turned in his chair, his dark eyes sad.

"I have something I need to tell you. I should have told you a long time ago."

Dorian took a deep breath.

"She's alive, Robert."

Robert stared at him, uncomprehending.

"She didn't die on that battlefield, all those years ago," Dorian continued. "We – I – made a mistake."

Robert listened to Dorian's confession with horror, and then a wash of memory took him over so that it seemed as if the selkie did not speak at all.

***

The old pub was still there, but now Robert was rich. Everyone paid attention, and the crowd was full of appreciative spectators, many of whom were women. No one shouted at him, or cursed. He was his country's national poet, and his confidence shone in his upright bearing.

He stood in front of the crowd, confident and collected. Handsome, his face and body filled out with the food and drink he could now afford, he wore his new red tailcoat well.

His words flowed much like the river they described, and although the pub was full, they were for one person alone, who was not even in attendance.

"On Cessnock banks a lassie dwells;
Could I describe her shape and mien;
Our lasses a' she far excels,
 An' she has twa sparkling roguish een.

She's sweeter than the morning dawn,
When rising Phoebus first is seen,
And dew-drops twinkle o'er the lawn;
An' she has twa sparkling roguish een.

She's stately like yon youthful ash,
That grows the cowslip braes between,
And drinks the stream with vigour fresh;
An' she has twa sparkling roguish een."

Desdemona was not present that evening, and would often be absent in his life, and his afterlife – and yet, to him, she was everything. He remembered her, talking with him, laughing, fighting alongside him, and he knew there would not be another like her, in this world or the next.

He touched his shirt cuffs briefly, an old habit, and smiled a secret smile, because no one would, or could, ever know.

"But it's not her air, her form, her face,
Tho' matching beauty's fabled queen;
'Tis the mind that shines in ev'ry grace,
An' chiefly in her roguish een."

***

The lights on Kelvinbridge were orange, the summer night warm and welcoming. Robert walked up the escalator of the subway station and turned to the left, knowing he was heading in the direction of her club, and not knowing what to feel. His mind and heart were a tumult of emotion.

And in front of him, he saw a woman with long, ginger hair, lighting a cigarette beneath a street lamp.

Desdemona.

He would know her anywhere, in any form.

She turned, her eyes green and bright, even in the darkness. She breathed smoke that coiled around her

174

body like a lover, like the first night they met and she took his hand to lead him into a fantastic world of faeries and monsters.

He stood in front of her, lost for words.

And Desdemona waited.

The End